The

with the

Walled Garden

CLAIRE CAREY

Claire Carey

01-01-24

THE CLOISTER HOUSE PRESS

First published in the United Kingdom in 2021 by
The Cloister House Press

ISBN 978-1-913460-33-4

Contents

Thank you to India Danter
for your excellent cover artwork.

Thank you to my editor Meg Humpries,
I consider myself lucky to be able to
work with you.

And last a thank you to all the team at
The Choir Press for your continued support.

Max

There once lived a secret man who liked to live a quiet life. He looked after a walled garden. Everybody knew the secret man as 'the gardener', and when he was not tending to the walled garden he would look after the gardens of everyone else in our village. The gardener was a very nice man with a kind heart. He had lived in our village before anybody else. The gardener had no family that we knew of, and his main job was to supply our local shop with the freshest fruit and vegetables possible, and the sweetest-smelling flowers money could buy, from the walled garden. Now, let me tell you a story about how anything can happen.

The walled garden was the best thing about our village. Although it was shrouded in mystery and secrets, it was very useful. The gardener would work day and night, making sure that walled garden grew the best grapes, tomatoes, potatoes, oranges, apples, pears, carrots, peas, cauliflower and broccoli. The gardener, as if by magic, had even found a way to grow pineapples, bananas and coconuts – there wasn't anything that he couldn't grow. The gardener also grew the best flowers, everything from roses to lilies and carnations of all colours. Fresh herbs too, there was no end to the gardener's talent. The walled garden was very useful and the gardener made sure everything was as good as it could be. As far as we knew,

1

nobody had ever seen inside the walled garden. We'd only ever seen the produce it grew.

There was also another side to the garden that nobody mentioned. On that side, there was a witch who owned and helped to look after the walled garden. The witch was also the gatekeeper because within the walled garden there was said to be a secret gate, and the witch held the key to this gate. The witch was known to be a very wise woman, and it was said that she locked the secret gate many years ago and declared herself the gatekeeper so nobody could enter through the secret gate. The secret gate had a very tragic secret. The witch would watch over the gardener and garden to make sure nobody could get in the garden, only the gardener. Many, many years ago, nearly everybody in our village, at different times, had tried to break into the walled garden when the gardener was away. The gardener had a little caravan and he would go off for a few days and nobody knew where he went or when he'd return. It was said that for many years the witch was feared because for some reason she cast a complete spell on our village. Our parents never spoke of the walled garden nor did they let us go near it. But that all changed when Grandma Daisy visited.

My name is Max, and my little village is just outside Cambridge. Our village is so small that we only have one shop, one pub, one post box, one phone box, one walled garden, one way in and one out. I have one brother and one sister, that's Kelvin, who's fifteen, Jazz, who's thirteen, and me, aged twelve. Kelvin is autistic and we call him the timekeeper because he loves clocks – our study downstairs is full of clocks. Kelvin can tell you the time anywhere in the world at any minute of the day. This had all started with a visit to London because Mum wanted to hear the chimes of Big Ben, and Kelvin was so impressed that he's been keeping time ever since. Yazz likes to play the piano and tells us that when she is old enough she is going to work in theatre land in London. Dad tells Jazz she had better be good and work hard because London is a very expensive place to live. Fashion is my favourite subject – I enjoy everything about fashion: fabrics, shoes, belts, hats, dresses and suits. I admire Thomas Burberry and Paul Smith, both British-born top designers and manufacturers. I intended to follow in their footsteps. I intend to design and make fabrics that were fashionable and robust, long-lasting. Dad told me I would have to move up north because apparently that was where most textiles are made in the UK.

Mum is a stay-at-home mum because our house is very old and needs a lot of upkeep, so it's great for us, because Mum is always at home. Mum loves Dad, Dad loves us and we all love Mum and Dad. Our dad is a military man, in the Royal Navy, and can be gone for weeks at any one time. We all miss him very much when he is away, but I think Mum misses him the most.

One day, just before school, Dad called us all into the living room. 'Now then, children, your mum and I are going away for five days. That means Grandma Daisy is coming to take care of you three, so you'd better be on your best behaviour. Grandma Daisy will pick you up after school because we will have left by the time school has finished. So please all stay together and Grandma will pick you up from the main entrance.'

Because Kelvin is autistic Mum and Dad have to make sure he understands everything and knows that his daily routine will not be affected so as not to cause Kelvin any stress. As long as his routine is not disturbed, Kelvin is fine and copes very well. Grandma Daisy is very good with Kelvin – she has always been there for him since he was born to help my mum whenever she needed extra support. When Yazz and I were little, Kelvin would also spend most weekends with Grandma Daisy because he liked to have his own space, peace and quiet away from me and Jazz. But now we are all older, Kelvin likes to be with us. Kelvin and I share a bedroom, but there is a line down the middle of the room so I cannot put any of my stuff on Kelvin's side of the room. I do my best to keep the room very tidy so I don't upset Kelvin, and Kelvin knows this, so we get on very well. And in return, Kelvin is not allowed to have any clocks in our bedroom, because their ticking would keep me awake at night, so all of Kelvin's clocks are downstairs in the study. Kelvin has one clock for every time zone in the world and one clock for every country in the world. Although Kelvin is very independent and his autism is very manageable, Jazz and I have always looked out for him. Ever since I can remember, our mum and dad have made sure we are aware that Kelvin just needs a little more support than me and Jazz, so we've always done what we can to make sure Kelvin is happy. We are very lucky that Kelvin attends the same school as me and Jazz.

After school, we all met outside at the main entrance as Dad instructed us to do, and Grandma Daisy was waiting for us. Grandma was very pleased to see us, all big hugs and kisses. We all jumped into Grandma's car and made for home. Once we arrived home Grandma made us all a cup of tea and we sat at the kitchen table, talking about all the things we had been up to since we last saw Grandma. I could see Grandma was very happy to be spending time with us, and us with Grandma. After our cup of tea, Grandma suggested we all have a walk down to the shop and get something nice for tea. 'And maybe,' Grandma said, 'I might bump into some old friends.'

We all went upstairs and changed out of our school uniforms and folded them up tidily ready for the next day, and changed our shoes and off to the shop we all went. On the way to the shop, just as Grandma had suggested, she bumped into some old friends. Mr Grey was the first person we bumped into.

'Hello, Daisy. Long time no see. How are you keeping?'

'Very well thank you, Fred. And you how are you keeping?'

'Can't complain. I'm keeping busy – that's the most important thing these days, keeping active. How long are you visiting for?'

'Well, Fred, I'm going to be staying for a few days. You should come round we can have a catch-up.'

'I will do that, Daisy.'

'Yes,' said Daisy, 'Come around about eleven tomorrow.'

'Yes, that would be lovely. See you then.'

Grandma was very happy to see Fred. Grandma explained to us that Fred was Grandad Jim's best friend, and she was looking forward to seeing Fred to have a talk about old times. The next person we bumped into was Mrs Khan. Mrs Khan was like Mary Poppins everything perfect.

'Hello, Daisy, nice to see and you.'

'And you, Naga. You look very well, if you don't mind me saying.'

'That's very kind of you, Daisy.'

Grandma explained to Mrs Khan that she'd just seen Fred and that he was coming round for a cup of tea the next day at eleven would she like to join us.

'Oh yes please. That would be very nice, thank you,' said Mrs Khan.

'Okay, see you tomorrow,' replied Grandma.

We finally arrived at the shop, and Mr and Mrs Fudge, the shopkeepers, were very pleased to see our grandma.

Hello, Daisy are you back?

'Yes, but only for a few days. My Tom and Lillie have gone away, so I have the job of looking after these three monkeys.'

Mr Fudge looked at us and said, 'Daisy, you are very much mistaken. They are not monkeys.' We all started to laugh. 'Very good children, your Tom's children. Always polite when they visit our shop, isn't that right, May?'

'Yes, John, very nice children, all three of them.'

My Grandma had a very proud smile on her face. 'Thank you, it's very pleasing to hear such nice comments.'

Mr Fudge replied, 'Well, you know me, Daisy. If they were naughty, I would not allow them into my shop.'

'Yes, I know you, John,' replied Grandma, 'and I wouldn't blame you.'

Mr Fudge told Grandma that it was almost a full moon. 'So,' he added', 'you know who may well be visiting soon.'

Grandma replied, 'Yes, and I don't suppose we will get to see her.'

'No,' said Mrs Fudge. 'We definitely won't see her.'

I couldn't help listening to the conversation, and without thinking I said to Mrs Fudge, 'Who you are talking about?'

Mrs Fudge replied, 'Witch Matilda.'

'Who?' I quickly asked. 'Is that her name?'

'Yes,' replied Mr Fudge. 'Matilda is a very wise woman. If you are lucky enough to meet her, you we never forget her.'

'I would love to meet her someday.'

'Right,' Grandma said. 'We'd best get moving, otherwise tea will turn into supper.'

Grandma picked up a few things and we left.

'Don't stay away too long, Daisy,' said Mrs Fudge.

Grandma replied, 'I will see you tomorrow – I will be back in. I'm having a few around for tea at 11 a.m. if you would like to join us.'

'We would love to, but we cannot leave the shop.' Mr and Mrs Fudge never left the shop, not even to go on holiday – their shop was their life, and a very good job they did too.

On our return home, Grandma noticed that the gardener's caravan was gone.

The gardener's away, by the looks of things,' said Grandma.

'Yes, he left late last night,' said Kelvin. 'I saw him leaving around 21.00 hours, which was 23.00 in Athens in Greece.'

'You sound just like your father, Kelvin,' said Grandma.

I asked Grandma, as I had done many times before, 'Can you tell us some more stories about the gardener?'

Grandma replied, 'Yes, he is very old, and the gardener lived in the village before anybody else. He is a very nice man, but a very secret man.'

Yazz asked Grandma, 'Do you know his name?'

'No, I'm afraid not. I only know him as the gardener.'

Kelvin asked Grandma, 'Do you know how old he is?'

'No, only that he is very old, and works very hard. I think that's what keeps him going – hard work.'

Yazz asked Grandma, 'Does he have any children?'

'Not, to my knowledge,' Grandma said. 'He is a real living secret.'

I asked Grandma, 'Have you ever been into the walled garden?'

Grandma replied, 'No, but I always wanted to.'

Grandma told us that if we could meet the gatekeeper, we could go into the walled garden, but if we tried to break in, the nettles were so strong that if they stung you, the pain would last for the rest of your life.

Yazz told Grandma that she really wanted to visit the walled garden, and Grandma replied, 'Yes, you and many more would love to see inside the walled garden, but we need permission from the gatekeeper.'

I asked, 'Who is the gatekeeper?'

Grandma told us that the Witch Matilda is the gatekeeper and that she had the keys to the walled garden and the secret gate.

I asked Grandma, 'Do you know where witch Matilda lives?'

'Yes,' said Grandma. 'She lives on the most eastern part of the UK, a little place called Horsey Gap.'

We all started to laugh.

'Horsey Gap! That's a funny name!' I chuckled.

'Yes, you are right, Max, it is a funny name. However, that is roughly the most easterly part of the UK, and it's there that the witch Matilda lives in an alcazar, which is a type of palace.'

I asked Grandma, 'Can we go to Horsey Gap to see the witch Matilda in her alcazar please?'

'Not today, Max,' replied Grandma.

I asked, 'Will the witch Matilda be visiting the walled garden?'

Grandma replied, 'Yes, the witch Matilda will visit the day after a full moon, which is roughly twelve times every year, and she also likes to visit if the gardener is away.'

Yazz asked, 'Is the witch Matilda nice?'

Grandma said, 'Rumour has it that she is a very nice, and very beautiful, but you must not upset the witch.'

'Beautiful?' I said. 'But every witch I've ever seen has been green and not very kind on the eyes.'

Yazz replied, 'Don't you mean ugly?'

'Yes, Yazz, but I'm trying to put it nicely.'

Grandma replied, 'Yes, but sometimes not everything is what you would imagine it to be or how you would imagine it to look.'

I asked Grandma, 'Has the witch Matilda got a broomstick?'

Grandma replied, 'The witch would not be a witch if she never had a broomstick, I'm sure. Every witch must have a broomstick.'

By then, we were home, and Grandma started to make the tea. Grandma loved to cook for us. She was a very good cook, and I always looked forward to Grandma's cooking.

I asked Grandma, 'What are we having for tea?'

Grandma replied, 'Toad in the hole.'

'Yummy!'

About an hour later, Grandma sat us all down at the kitchen table for tea. It was delicious and there wasn't a single crumb left. When we were at the shop, Grandma bought a chocolate cake, so next on the menu was chocolate cake and ice cream.

After tea, Kelvin and Yazz cleaned up, and Grandma went into the living room put on the TV, then fell asleep. I had homework to do, so I got stuck in. Once Kelvin and Yazz had cleaned up, Grandma woke up. As it was still light outside and warm, we all went into the garden.

Our garden backs onto the walled garden with just a small road in between. We were all still very keen to know more stories about the walled garden, trying to make the most of Grandma's knowledge, and Grandma loved telling us stories about the garden.

I asked, 'Do you think the witch Matilda will visit the walled garden soon?'

'Most probably, when the gardener is away, or the day after the full moon.' Grandma looked straight over at me and noticed I had a smile on my face from ear to ear. 'Clever child, you are, Max.'

This made me feel hopeful that I would get to meet the witch. For what reason would I feel like that? It just felt so exciting knowing that the gardener was away. Grandma must have realised what I was thinking when she saw the look on my face. 'Now, Max,' she said with a big smile on her face, 'don't get any ideas.'

I could not wait to tell Kelvin and Yazz what I'd discovered. I went skipping down the garden – I could hardly get my breath I was so excited – to inform Kelvin and Yazz that the witch Matilda only visits the walled garden when the gardener was away or the day after a full moon. I could see by the look on their faces that Kelvin and Yazz felt as excited as I did.

Kelvin looked at me and said, 'Are you telling stories, Max?'

'No, honestly, it's true. Grandma as just told me.'

Yazz and I were jumping up and down and laughing with excitement.

Grandma came walking down the garden. 'Now then, what is going on here?'

Yazz replied, 'Max has just told us that the witch Matilda visits the walled garden when the gardener is away or the day after a full moon. Is this true?'

Daisy could see how excited the children were at

knowing the gardener was away. 'I think we all need to calm down, children. Just because the gardener is away, this doesn't mean we will see the witch.'

'But Grandma,' said Yazz, 'you said that if the gardener is away the witch Matilda will visit.'

'That's right,' said Grandma. 'However, in all the years I've lived in the village, I've never seen the witch Matilda.'

'Why not?' I asked.

'For many years, the witch Matilda was feared.'

'Why was she feared?' I asked.

'Because she is a witch, and many years ago the witch put a spell on the entire village so that everybody would always fear the witch.'

Kelvin asked Grandma, 'Why would the witch put a spell on the village?'

'Well, many years ago, most people from the village had tried to break into the walled garden. As you know, the gardener has always warned the villagers to stay away from the walled garden because of the secret gate. Well, a long time ago the largest man with the biggest hammer had been trying very hard to break into the walled garden, and he had been hitting the wall all day until he broke his wrist. The man was in so much pain that he could not hit the wall any more. Unbeknown to the largest man, he knocked some of the stone out of the wall on the inside. When the gardener returned with his caravan the next morning, he went into the walled garden as normal and discovered that some of the stone was missing from the wall. When he went over to where the stone was missing, the missing stone lay on the ground. The gardener then tried to repair the wall by putting the stone back into place, but the stone was very heavy and as he tried to lift the stone, he lost his balance, fell to the ground and let go of the stone. As the gardener fell, the stone landed on his head and knocked him out, and of course, nobody knew. The next day, Mr Fudge waited for the gardener to make his delivery – and waited and waited. Mr Fudge knew that something was not right, because the gardener was always on time.

'How did the witch find out?' Kelvin asked.

'Mr Fudge and the birds in the trees carried the message back to her. Mr Fudge followed the birds to Horsey Gap, and the witch came to the gardener's rescue.

'What happened to the gardener after that?' asked Yazz.

'He needed to spend several weeks in hospital to recover. The witch was very angry with everybody in the village. She was so upset that in all her anger she put a spell on the village.'

The three of us were completely silent, mouths open.

'I don't understand,' I said. 'Why would the witch put a spell on everybody?'

Grandma replied, 'Because the witch was very disappointed with everybody who had tried to break into the garden, and she wanted everybody in the village to know what the biggest man with the biggest hammer had done.

'What happened after that?' Yazz said, wide-eyed.

'It's a long story, and it was before I married your Grandad Jim and I moved into the village, and if I'm honest I cannot remember all the details – I only know that the village got filled up with nettles. Grandad Jim was very strict with your father when it came to the walled garden. He would never let him go near it, not even stand near the wall. I could never understand why. I never feared the walled garden. Perhaps that's because I wasn't around when the spell took place. I think we will have to finish this tomorrow after school.'

I replied, 'But we really want to know what happened next!'

'Yes,' said Grandma, 'and I really want to tell you, but I will have to think about it so that I get the story correct. It's many years ago, so I need time to remember, and it's getting late, so let's leave it there until tomorrow.'

I sighed and shrugged my shoulders. 'Okay.' 'It's time for bed now, children, and I think you should start getting ready for bed. School in the morning.'

'We love hearing about the walled garden,' Yazz frowned.

'Yes, I know,' replied Grandma, 'so we will carry on tomorrow.'

We reluctantly went upstairs and put ourselves to bed. At just after ten we heard Grandma creep upstairs to make sure we were all in bed – and of course, we were all still wide awake, and Yazz was in our room as we all chattered excitedly.

Grandma put an arm around Yazz's shoulder, starting to guide her out to her own room. 'Yazz, it's bedtime. Come on, now, get to bed, and try to settle down and get some sleep.'

'I can't, Grandma! I really want to visit the walled garden. I think I would like to meet the witch,' said Yazz.

Grandma replied, 'I've lived in this village for many years and never been in the walled garden and never seen the witch.'

Yazz replied, 'Yes, Grandma, but things have changed, and the gardener is getting very old. The witch may well need someone else to look after the garden for her.'

'Yes, that might be the case someday, but not tonight, Yazz, so try to settle down.'

'Okay,' replied Yazz. 'I will try. Good night, Grandma.'

'Good night, Yazz.'

Yazz shuffled off to bed, leaving just Kelvin and me with Grandma. We were now standing by the window, looking at the walled garden.

'Grandma! Grandma!' I shouted. Look, it's nearly a full moon!'

Grandma walked over to the window and looked up at the moon. 'Oh yes,' she replied. 'Maybe tomorrow night will be a full moon.'

'And the day after that the witch will visit?'

'Just maybe, Max. Just maybe.'

Kelvin said, 'Yes, and at 21.05, if it's a clear night, we should be able to see the moon.'

'Look, Grandma! We can see light coming from the walled garden!' I exclaimed.

Grandma said, 'Yes, look at that. The gardener must have come home. Now then, boys, it's definitely time for bed.'

'Okay, Grandma,' we both replied. 'Good night.'

The children struggled to sleep. Grandma's visit had cast a new light on the walled garden. We were totally enthralled by the story our grandma had told us, and we wanted to know more and more about the walled garden. It was as if the walled garden was fast becoming magnetic to us, as if it was drawing us in. Kelvin and I could not sleep – we were chatting for most of the night, even though we had tried very hard to get to sleep. The light that came from the walled garden that night seemed to be getting brighter and brighter as the night went on.

Yazz also struggled to get to sleep, she told us the next day. She couldn't see the walled garden from her room, but still, Grandma's story rattled round in her head. The next morning, Grandma struggled to wake us all up and found us all fast asleep.

'Oh, I am sorry, children,' Grandma said as she started to put breakfast on the table. 'I think we talked too much about the walled garden yesterday.'

'Yes, but Grandma, we love to hear about the garden, and we only get to hear about it when you visit. Mum and Dad never mention the walled garden to us.'

Grandma replied, 'And I know why.' Before I could ask why, she continued, 'Will you be okay to go to school today?'

Yazz said, 'Yes, Grandma. Don't worry, we will all be fine.'

'Not me,' I yawned. 'I'm sooooo tired, Grandma.'

'Well, Max, if you fall asleep, I will come and pick you up.'

'But I'm falling asleep now, Grandma.'

Grandma shook her head and laughed. 'Just try, Max, please. Otherwise, your parents will not let me look after you again.'

'That's right,' said Yazz. 'Do your best, Max.'

I sighed. 'Okay.'

Grandma said, 'That's the spirit. Chin up, Max.'

I asked Grandma, 'When we get back from school, can you tell us some more stories about the walled garden?'

Grandma replied, 'Yes, of course, and I will have more stories after my friends have been round to see me. Fred has lived in the village all his life, and he will remember everything about the spell that the witch cast upon the village.'

Yazz said, 'I will look forward to hearing some more stories.'

'Okay, children. Eat up your breakfast. It's nearly time to leave.'

'Yes,' said Kelvin, 'it's 08.15 a.m. and we need to be in

the car by 8.20 a.m. to leave, so that we arrive on time at 8.42 a.m. That will leave us exactly three minutes before the bell goes. And that means in Mumbai right now it's exactly 13.15 p.m., and in Baltimore, Maryland, USA it's exactly 03.15 a.m.'

'You amaze me, Kelvin,' said Grandma. 'How you remember all that I will never know. You are such a clever young man.'

Kelvin smiled and nodded.

We finished our breakfast, picked up our bags and then Grandma drove us to school at exactly the right time so as not to upset Kelvin.

On the way to school, I noticed that the gardener's caravan was not there when we passed his house. So, who was in the garden last night? I wondered if it was the witch. As I looked over to Yazz, I could see that she had also noticed that the gardener's caravan was not there. Kelvin also seemed to be deep in thought, probably thinking back to the night before and wondering why the walled garden was lit up so brightly – did the gardener come home and then leave again early this morning before anybody noticed? It looked like he had been and gone. I really needed to solve this mystery.

We arrived at school right on time, and Grandma made sure we had everything and told us to stay together once we came out of school so she could pick us up. Then she watched us until we were inside the school building.

Daisy

❦

Daisy arrived back at the house, cleaned up all the breakfast dishes, wiped the table, quickly got everything ready for Fred and Naga to arrive. Right on cue at 11 a.m., Naga arrived, followed by Fred.

'Come in, sit down. Tea or coffee?' Daisy asked.

They both replied, 'Tea, please.'

Naga had made a cake. 'How very thoughtful,' said Daisy. 'It's lovely to see you both again.'

Naga said, 'Thanks for inviting us.'

'I don't get many invitations these days,' said Fred. 'I still miss your Jim.'

'And me,' Daisy nodded with a sad smile. 'But tell you what, it's lovely to be back in the village.'

Fred asked, 'Do you ever consider moving back, Daisy?'

'I would love to move back into the village, but I have not been able to find a place that's suitable for me. I really miss living here. There is a great sense of community, and you can't find that everywhere.'

'This village is special,' Fred replied. 'We have the witch to thank for that.'

'Yes, that's right,' said Naga. 'The witch was right to put the spell on the village, although I didn't think that at the time. Since the spell, nobody ever tries to break into the garden, and everybody is more polite towards each other.'

Daisy said, 'I started telling the children about the spell

17

the witch put over the village last night, but they got so excited, and it was nearly time for bed, then they couldn't sleep. I felt so guilty this morning when they really struggled to get out of bed.'

Fred replied, 'Yes, Daisy, but they must be aware of the dangers that the walled garden can hold.'

Yes, that's right,' said Naga. 'Let's not forget what we have already learnt it is our duty to pass on our knowledge to the younger generations.'

Fred said, 'Nobody seems to move away from the village.'

'That's right,' said Daisy. 'I only moved because I couldn't manage the upkeep on this house. My Tom did ask me to stay, but I needed my privacy, and with three children in the house I knew that would not work for me. I love all three of them with all my heart and I would do anything for them, they bring me so much joy, but I cannot keep up the pace. When I'm away, I miss them terribly. If I had my own place in the village, that would work perfectly.'

Naga replied, 'Well, that is understandable.'

'How are the children?' asked Fred.

'They are all doing well but growing up to fast. They are fascinated with the walled garden.'

Naga replied, 'Same as the rest of us. I would love to step inside the walled garden.'

'Me and your Jim nearly did,' Fred said.

Daisy looked over to Fred with astonishment. 'Please tell!'

'Didn't your Jim ever tell you about our almost-visit to the walled garden?'

'No, he never mentioned that – not that I can remember, anyway,' replied Daisy. 'We would often talk about the walled garden, and Jim would say it was full of magic, and I never really understood what he meant. The witch Matilda is the best person to look after the walled garden – and the gardener, of course.'

'So, how did you and my Jim manage to almost visit the inside of the walled garden?'

'It's a long story,' Fred replied.

'We have all day,' said Naga.

'Okay, then. We were here, back when it was Jim's parent's house, playing outside the back of the house alongside the walled garden on the little road. Well, as you both know, Jim and I grew up in the village, and we were only young at this time – I was ten and Jim was eleven. We were playing with the football, taking turns, seeing how high we could kick the ball. On Jim's turn, he kicked the ball really high, and at the same time, a gust of wind came and took the ball over the wall and into the garden. Jim went white. I can see the look on his face now – he was horrified. "Fred," he said, "I need to get my ball back. My father will be very cross with me." I told Jim, "Don't worry, we will get the ball back." "But how? We cannot go into the walled garden." "No, but we can wait until the gardener goes in and ask the gardener if he can get the ball back." "Good idea," said Jim.

So we walked up to the gardener's house and waited and waited, but the gardener never came back to his house, so after about an hour we knocked on his door, but there was no answer. By then, Jim was getting very upset. I told Jim we could try again the next day, said, "Don't worry, I'm sure we'll get your football back tomorrow." Jim was very worried in case his father found out the ball was in the walled garden. Jim said, "My dad will not be worried about the ball, just the fact that it has gone into the walled garden." Then Jim suggested that we didn't mention the ball to his parents – it was agreed.

That night, I was staying over at Jim's because it was Friday, and Jim's dad was taking us both fishing the next day. We went up to bed and much to my surprise, the walled garden was lit up. There was a magnificent array of colours coming from the garden, and the light was so bright, the brightest light that I had ever seen. Although I had lived in the village all my life, this was the first time that I had ever seen the garden lit up. Jim had seen it many times before because his house backed onto the walled garden, so he didn't take too much notice. "The gardener must still be working," said Jim. "Maybe that's why he never returned to his house." I stared, awestruck. "Jim, look at the light – it is magnificent." "Yes it is," he agreed, "but it holds a lot of secrets, and my parents have always warned me to stay away. Because we live so close, I've seen the lights many times before." "Can we go and explore?" I asked Jim. "What, tonight?" said Jim. "Yes, let's go and take a look around the garden outside." "My parents will not be pleased with us if we go outside after dark!"

I said to Jim, "If we wait until they go to bed, and go quietly, they will never know we went out."

Jim didn't like the idea and was very reluctant about going out, but he agreed.

"Do you know the stories about the walled garden, Fred?" he asked.

I replied that I did. In truth, I didn't know all the stories, but I was very aware that we needed to keep out of the garden, but then we weren't going to go inside the garden anyway. "Let's just have a look around the outside and we might see the gardener and we can ask him to get your ball," I answered.

"I will be in big trouble if my parents find out."

I told Jim not to worry. "Your parents will not catch us. We will be as quiet as church mice."

Jim asked, "What do you mean?"

"We will not make a sound – tiptoe all the way."

Jim was still very reluctant, but like me he was curious. As we approached the walled garden I felt like a magnetic force was pulling me in towards the garden. It's hard to explain, but it's the same feeling you get as a child, knowing Santa has been, and your presents are just waiting to be unwrapped, the excitement of not knowing what's inside. Although Jim was not feeling the same as me, he'd seen the lights from the garden many times before.'

Naga asked, 'What happened next?'

'We managed to get out of the house without Jim's parents seeing or hearing us. Once we were outside, it was amazing – the light and the fresh smell felt so powerful.'

'Powerful?' asked Daisy. 'How?'

'Because it was magical, and I felt magical. The atmosphere was like something amazing was going to happen. The sense of excitement was taking over me, and once I was out, there was no way I was going back indoors anytime soon. Jim said, "I don't like this, let's go back inside." I replied, "No, let's go round to the gate – come on, Jim, don't be afraid, nothing can hurt us out here." I was not going back indoors until I'd had a good look around. I couldn't understand why Jim was so afraid. "Fred," he said, "please let's just go back inside. This doesn't feel right." But I didn't want to. I told Jim, "You can go back indoors, but I'm staying out here." Jim replied, "I'm not leaving you on your own." "We are out here now, Jim. Let's just go round to the gate and see if we can see the gardener and ask him if he can find your ball, then we will go back indoors." Jim reluctantly followed me, but I could see that he was really afraid of the walled garden. We needed to walk back up to the gardener's house and follow the gardener's private path down to the gate of the walled garden. Nobody except the gardener used the private path, so nobody had ever bothered to look at the gardener's path before – why would they? It only leads to the walled garden and nobody is allowed in the garden. When we got to the path, it was a beautiful shade of purple. It felt like magic! It was all glistening in the light of the moon. Both me and Jim stood looking at the purple path. Eventually, I asked Jim, "Did you know this path is purple?" "No," said Jim, "I've never seen this before. I never knew the gardener had a purple path." It looked too nice to walk on. It was all shiny, as if we would be the first two people to ever set foot on it. Standing at the top of the purple path looking down at the gate to the walled garden, I really wanted to walk down the path. It looked like a magic path, as if it had just landed, for me and Jim to walk down. Jim said, "Come on now, Fred. We have seen enough." I suppose, looking back now all these years later, Jim was more intelligent than me. He sensed danger that I never sensed, while I just wanted to put one foot on the path to see what it would feel like. As I put my one foot onto the path, my foot lit up. "Look at me, Jim!" I said, and before I realised what I was doing, I was standing with both feet on the path, and I was completely lit up, glowing like the moon. I just couldn't help myself – I started to walk down the purple path. I could feel that magnetic feeling again. Magic, it was, as if you couldn't turn back, so I took a few more steps down, and a few more – I couldn't stop myself. I turned around to look at

Jim, and he was not there, so I called, "Jim? Where are you?" He shouted back, "I'm not coming with you." I turned cold and for the first time, I could feel the fear that Jim felt. The magic feeling had gone and now a dark feeling came over me like a cloud. I just wanted to be standing next to Jim. The cold feeling of fear was making me shake – but I wasn't just shaking – I felt like I was rattling and I was shaking so much that I quickly turned around and started to walk back up the path towards the gardener's house ... but it was as if the purple path were pulling me towards the gate of the walled garden, and the faster I ran, the more I felt like I was sliding down. I shouted, "Jim! Help me! I'm sliding down!" Jim was standing at the top of the purple path. He held out his hands to me, but I couldn't reach them, so Jim laid down on the ground and reach out to me again. By then I was so anxious. I fell down onto the purple path and reach my hands up to Jim's, but I still couldn't reach Jim. I felt like I wasn't going to get back to the top. I could see Jim was very worried. The look of fear on his face worried me even more. I managed to crawl on my hands and knees, just enough for Jim to reach me. Once he reached my hands, he pulled me up, but it took all Jim's strength to do that. We managed to get far enough away for the sliding magnetic feeling to go away, and as we both looked round, the path seemed to go dark, like it was disappearing. As we turned around to look back at the gate of the walled garden, at that moment the gate opened. Now we were both very afraid and shaking – but I wasn't sure whether it was the cold, the fear, or both. For the first time that night, Jim stood tall and very calm. As the door opened, we could see inside ... and it looked magnificent. I had never seen anything like it: an array of colours. I could just see the apples on the tree – they were so beautiful, and they glowed like lightbulbs. I saw roses of all colours too. Jim was looking down in amazement – but that's when we noticed the shadow of the gardener walking towards the gate with his wheelbarrow. I said to Jim, "Quick, let's go!" Much to my surprise, Jim said, "No, we have come this far. Now the gardener is in sight, so I would like to ask the gardener if he has seen my ball." Jim was very stern in his tone of voice. I sensed he'd had enough of me and my exploring and that I'd caused enough trouble. As we looked back down towards the gate of the walled garden, the gardener was just closing the gate, and as the gardener pushed the gate shut, there was an almighty bang, and I felt the vibration on the ground as the gate closed, and then the noise of the keys clanging together as the gardener locked up the gate. It seemed to get very dark once the gardener locked the gate, and the only light left was the moonlight. The gardener turned around, picked up his barrow and started to walk up the purple path towards us. We were still trying to catch our breath, and I felt too weak to stand. As the gardener got to the top of the path, he raised his head and looked straight at Jim, and then nodded and looked at his barrow, so we also looked down at the barrow, and there in the barrow was the ball. The gardener smiled at Jim, nodded again, as if he was telling him to pick up his ball. Jim slowly picked up the ball and said, "Thank you very much, sir." The gardener smiled at Jim and said, "You know that if you try and get into the walled garden, the witch will get very angry with you both." Jim replied very hesitantly, "Yes, sir." "And this path," the gardener continued. "Please do not try to use this unless you have my permission. You have both been very lucky tonight, so let that be a warning to you." Jim explained, "My mum and dad have warned me to stay away from the walled garden." "Well, in that case, make sure you listen and learn to do what your parents tell you," the gardener said. Then he turned and looked at me and said, "Fred, you must not take this warning lightly. The witch is very nice, but she will not tolerate anybody trying to get into the walled garden." I couldn't stop myself from asking why. The gardener replied, "Because there is a secret gate within the walled garden, and many years ago two children went through the secret gate and never returned, and their family was devastated at the loss of their children. The mum and dad, and the grandparents never recovered, and that is why the witch is the gatekeeper and protector of the walled garden." Jim said, "But it looks so beautiful." "It is," said the gardener. "I've spent most of my life in the garden." I asked, "Do you think we will ever be able to go inside the walled garden?" The gardener replied, "The witch will not let anybody enter the walled garden until she knows she can trust you all again." Jim asked, "What is the witch's name?" "Matilda," replied the gardener. "Look, boys, it's very late, and you should be in bed." He looked at us and said, "Your mum and dad don't know you are out here, do they?" Jim put his head down and quietly said, "No, sir," so the gardener suggested, "In that case, it would be wise to quickly get back into your house before your parents realise that you are missing." We quietly made our way back to the house, unseen and unheard. Not long after our almost-visit to the walled garden, the witch cast a spell on the complete village.

It all started after the gardener came out of hospital. The witch was so angry that the gardener had been hurt, and the gardener was very upset that he couldn't tend to the walled garden until he fully recovered, and that was going to take months. So, in all her anger, the witch cast the spell and filled the walled garden with stinging nettles. Once they started to grow, they wouldn't stop until the spell was lifted, and that was going to take some doing. For the first few weeks nobody took any notice, then one morning somebody noticed that the nettles had reached the top of the walled garden, and we all know how tall the walls are. Within one month, the nettles were over the top and had started to trail down the outside of the wall. Everybody in the village started to take notice as the nettles grew longer and thicker. After about two months, the nettles were well on their way to the nearby houses. Some of the villagers had gotten very angry about the shop not being able to supply fresh fruit and vegetables from the walled garden, and soon the villagers were starting to get very cross with the people who had tried to break into the walled garden. A few weeks later, the villagers noticed that the nettles were starting to creep around their houses, and the road and footpaths. It was getting very tricky to navigate your way around the nettles, and you couldn't go out after dark. The villagers would cut them back but within days the nettles would grow back.'

Naga asked, 'How did they manage to get the spell lifted?'

'Well,' said Fred, 'that's another story, because they all knew that the witch was very upset and angry with villagers, and they needed to pull together to get the spell lifted, and they were unsure about just how to go about this. Some of the villagers organised a meeting in the village hall and urged everybody in the village to attend. I will never forget that night because all the children in the village attended as well. The meeting started, and everybody was coming up with different ideas to try and make the witch happy once again. One of the ladies suggested baking cakes, and another suggested painting the gardener's house and fence, and the suggestions went on and on. Nobody could agree on the best thing to do to make the witch happy again. And then, amongst all the disagreement, I remember there was one man who sat in the corner. He hadn't said anything, just sat there listening to everybody arguing. After a few hours, the gentleman stood up. He was tall, so he could see over the top of everybody else. He picked up his chair and banged on the floor very hard. Everybody in the hall went quiet and turned around to look at him. He calmly lifted his head and said to everybody in the room, 'Remember, you are all the problem. Everybody in this hall. It's all our fault.' The tall man then turned and pointed to all the children playing and said, 'Our village has lost all sense of community, and this has become a problem that only we ourselves can repair. We shouldn't have tried to break into the walled garden. The witch has every right to be angry with this village.' The tall man continued, 'You think baking cakes to make money will help, as if money is the cure. The gardener keeps the local shop full of fruit, vegetables and the best flowers even seen, so ask yourselves why. And the answer is always the same: because we are greedy, or because we are nosy, or because we want more than the person standing next to you.' Everybody was listening to the tall man. Even all the children had stopped playing to listen to the tall man. Some of the people in the hall had gone red with embarrassment, and some of them were standing with their heads down. 'So,' he went on to say, 'if we can stop the greediness and start trying to be more friendly towards each other, like our children are all having a good time in here tonight, why is that? Because they are all together. Nobody is entertaining them, they are just happy to be together and play. I'm sure the witch would be more than happy to lift the spell if we pulled together and organised a village fair and showed the witch that we still have respect for the walled garden, each other and the gardener.' Everybody in the hall stood up and gave the tall man a round of applause.

'You're right!' somebody shouted out to him.

'Thank you,' he replied, and with that, he sat back down. And so it was agreed that the village would have a big party on the village green.

Naga asked 'But how would that help lift the spell?'

'Well, we all found out years later that the witch had told the gardener that all the villagers were selfish, and all they were interested in was trying to upset the daily running of the walled garden. For their own greed, the spell was no less than they deserved, and until they could prove otherwise, until they could work together to make a better and more friendly village, the spell would remain, until the nettles had consumed the entire village, and then they would all have to move away. I'd learnt my lesson, and I never went near the walled garden again. The witch is very powerful, and it's best not to upset her. Nobody in the village ever tried again to break into the walled garden, and that's why our village has a good community.'

Daisy said, 'I can't believe I've never heard this before, but then again, Jim did tend to keep things to himself. Now, Fred, I could listen to you all today, but I'm afraid we will have to leave it there for today. It's time for me to crack on with a few jobs, then pick up the children.'

'Suits me,' Fred replied. 'I'm all talked out now, need a breather.'

Daisy gave her guests a peck on the cheek as they rose and headed for the door. 'It's been very nice to see you both – good god where has the time gone!'

'We must do it again,' said Fred.

'Ooh yes,' said Naga.

'Same time tomorrow, then?' said Daisy. 'I'll make some more cakes.'

'Good idea,' said Fred. 'Nothing like homemade cakes.'

Daisy needed to get her skates, she thought as she watched her friends walk down the path. Kelvin would get stressed if she wasn't on time.

Max

When Grandma arrived at the school, we were all already waiting outside.

'Hello, you three. Have you been waiting long?'

'No,' replied Yazz.

'Approximately two minutes and fifteen seconds,' said Kelvin.

'Well done, Kelvin,' said Grandma.

'Have you had a nice day, Grandma?' I asked.

'Yes, my friends came round as planned. We chatted and chatted.'

I quickly asked, 'Have you got any more stories about the walled garden?'

'Maybe,' Grandma winked. 'Perhaps after tea, and when you have done your homework, I will tell you all what Fred has told me today.'

As we got back to our village and we drove past the gardener's house, I noticed that the gardener's caravan wasn't there. I wondered to myself where he was, and whether he would be back that night.

I liked Grandma looking after us because she let us talk about the walled garden, and our parents never mentioned the garden, nor were we allowed to talk about it. Mum and Dad always discouraged any talk of the walled garden and always made sure we didn't go near it. But Grandma let us talk about the garden all the time. And if I'm honest, I wondered to myself if Mum and Dad knew that Grandma Daisy changed the rules when she stayed at our house. I also thought to myself how I wouldn't mention it to my Mum and Dad, just in case I got Grandma into trouble.

'Grandma! Grandma, did you notice that the gardener's caravan was not parked outside his house?'

'No,' she replied. 'No, I never noticed, Max,'

'Grandma, the caravan wasn't there, so that means that the gardener was not in the walled garden last night!'

Yazz said, 'Wait, so if the gardener wasn't in the garden last night, could that mean the witch was in the garden?'

Kelvin replied, 'What if the gardener came back last night at 11.35 p.m. and left early at 06.35 a.m. this morning before anybody noticed?'

Grandma said, 'You could be right there, Kelvin.'

Kelvin continued, 'I know that the gardener is not at home now, so tonight before I go to sleep I will check to see if his caravan has returned.'

Yazz said, 'That's spying!'

'Maybe,' said Kelvin, 'but I need to know. And if I check at 22.45 if the caravan is there, that is precisely fifteen minutes before you go to sleep, which equals 6.00 in Shenzhen Province in China.' Just then, we arrived home. Grandma suggested that we got our homework done whilst she prepared tea. I told Grandma that I didn't have any homework, even though I did.

'Are you sure, Max?'

'Yes, Grandma.'

Yazz went up to her bedroom to do her homework and Kelvin did the same.

'Grandma, it will take no less than forty-seven minutes and thirty seconds to get my homework done,' said Kelvin as he went up the stairs.

I went into the living room and put on the TV. Grandma made us all a cup of tea and once she'd taken Kelvin and Yazz's tea up to her bedrooms she came and sat in the living room with me. I drank my tea and then I must have fallen asleep. The next thing I remember was Grandma calling us for tea. Grandma had made spaghetti bolognese with parmesan cheese – delicious. After dinner, Grandma opened a tin of fruit salad and a tub of ice cream.

'Please can you tell us some more stories now about the garden?' I begged.

'We need to get the pots and pans cleared away first,' she said, so we all jumped up and within ten minutes everything was washed and packed away.

'Let the story begin!' said Yazz excitedly.

Grandma told us everything Fred had told her earlier that day, and we were gobsmacked the whole way through.

Kelvin asked, 'Why didn't those lost children come back after going through the secret gate?'

'The secret gate is a gateway between times,' Grandma explained. 'Once you walk through the gate, you have to be back on the other side at one minute past precisely, on the twelfth hour to which you arrived, and then you have a further four minutes to walk back through in order to get back to where you started.'

I ran Grandma's words around my head time and time again but they wouldn't click into place. The rules sounded like something from an old fairy tale.

Yazz said, 'So, the children are lost in time?'

'Yes, you could say that.'

I asked, 'Would they still be alive now?'

'It's hard to say, Max. Nobody knows.'

Kelvin said, 'They needed a timekeeper like me.'

Grandma said, 'Yes, Kelvin, I'm sure they wouldn't have gone missing if you'd been there.'

'Who were their parents?' Kelvin asked.

'It was many, many years ago, so nobody in the village knows, Kelvin.'

'Wait a minute!' I said. 'You told me that the gardener has lived in the village before anybody else, so could that mean that gardener did have children and they went missing, and that's why he's been looking after the garden ever since?'

Grandma frowned, then cocked her head, thinking hard.

'Are you okay, Grandma?' asked Yazz.

She paused for what felt like ages, and you could have heard a pin drop. Grandma's face told the story: she was in shock, with a look of horror on her face. We didn't know what to do. I kept apologising: 'I'm sorry, Grandma. I didn't mean to upset you.'

And then, after what seemed a lifetime, Grandma finally replied, 'It's not your fault, Max.' She had a sad tone of voice and a very sad look on her face. I looked over at Kelvin and I could see he was getting stressed, so Yazz said to Kelvin, 'Let's go into the study and see what time it is in Brazil.'

Kelvin replied, 'It's 20.07 here, so that means it's 00.07 in Belem, Brazil.'

'Grandma, why are you upset?' I asked once we were on our own.

Grandma replied, 'Because I lived in the village for many years, and never in all those years did I think that the gardener could have lost his children through the secret gate, and I've only ever mentioned the story to you once and you worked out a very good reason why the gardener has spent most of his life looking after the garden.

'Oh no, I didn't mean to upset you, Grandma!' I moaned.

'Oh Max, you haven't upset me. I just feel very sad for the gardener, because what you have said is a very logical explanation. And I feel very angry with myself for not getting to know the gardener better.'

'You didn't know, Grandma.'

'That's correct, and because I didn't know, I have never bothered to find out. The gardener is a very kind man – everybody in this village knows that – yet nobody has ever bothered to ask him about his life – so long as he was looking after the walled garden, we all thought he was okay.'

Once Grandma got herself back together, we both went into the study to make sure Kelvin was okay.

'Kelvin are you alright?' Grandma asked him.

'Yes, Grandma, I'm fine. Are you okay?'

'I am now, Kelvin.'

'It's very sad about the children going through the secret gate,' Kelvin went on to say. 'If I myself had been there, I would have made sure the children got back at the right time.'

'Yes, we would have definitely been able to rely on you to keep time, Kelvin.

'Yes, I would not have failed, Grandma.'

'I know, Kelvin. Now, it's getting late, so please can you all get ready for bed.'

Quietly and meekly, we did as she asked. We could see that Grandma was very upset at the possibility that the missing children were the gardener's children. Grandma never said any more about the garden that night, and we never asked any more questions, just cleaned our teeth and went to our rooms.

That night, the garden was lit up again, but we didn't mention it, nor did Grandma. While lying in bed, trying to drop off to sleep, I realised why our parents never mentioned the walled garden to us. Until that week I hadn't realised just how dangerous it could be. Before, we had never taken too much notice, because it had never crossed anybody's minds that the missing children could be anything to do with our village, or even that the event had actually taken place. However, I could see by the look on Grandma's face that for her this had become reality. I suppose over the many years of living in the village, Grandma had subconsciously gathered information, and now it was all coming together. I couldn't help but think about the gardener – no wonder he was such a quiet man. I imagine he would avoid contact with other people in case they asked too many questions that he would prefer not to answer.

That night, I was very restless. One minute I was asleep, and the next I was wide awake. At some point in the middle of the night, I decided to go downstairs and get a drink of water. When I got downstairs, Grandma was sitting in the living room looking at the garden, which was still lit up. Grandma still looked sad.

'Are you okay?' I asked her.

'Yes, I'm fine, love. It's been a long day and I couldn't sleep. Lots of things going through my mind. What are you doing up anyway?'

'I woke up and I was thirsty, so I'm just getting some water.'

I thought it best to leave Grandma to it, so I got my water and went back up to bed. I knew Grandma was sad because my suggestion about the lost children being the gardener's had really got her thinking.

The next morning, Kelvin's alarm clock went off at 07.00. Yesterday, we got woken up with a cup of tea, but no tea today. I knocked on Yazz's door to make sure she was awake.

'Yes, I'm awake!'

'Just checking!'

Then I went downstairs whilst Kelvin was using the bathroom – I always wash last. As I got downstairs, I saw Grandma, who was sound asleep on the settee. I looked in the spare room and saw that the bed was still made.

Just then, Yazz came downstairs. She looked at Grandma, raised her eyebrows at me, and put on the kettle to make a cup of tea. Grandma must have heard the kettle boiling and woke up.

'Good god!' she said. 'Is that the time? 7.20?'

'Yes, but don't worry, Grandma. We are all up.'

'Where's Kelvin?'

'He's washing,' said Yazz.'

'Thank god you're all up and getting ready for school. Such good children, you are.'

Yazz poured the tea. I noticed that Grandma looked happier.

'Cup of tea for me as well? This is the life,' sighed Grandma. 'What are we having for breakfast?'

Kelvin, now on his way down the stairs said, 'Can we have poached egg on toast?'

'Yes, of course,' Grandma smiled.

Grandma made us all breakfast and another cup of tea, and while we were eating breakfast, Grandma had a wash and got dressed. We all needed to be ready by 08.15 a.m., otherwise Kelvin would get stressed and start worrying about being late for school.

'Do you know,' said Kelvin, 'that it is approximately 07.45 a.m., which means that in Auckland, New Zealand, the time will be 17.45 p.m., so that tells me that as our working day starts, their working day is just coming to an end.'

We left for school right on cue at 08.20 a.m. and arrived at 08.42 a.m. Kelvin was happy and so were we. As I got out of the car, I turned and looked straight at Grandma and said, 'Will you be okay today, Grandma?

'Yes, Max, I will be fine.'

'I can come back home with you if you like?'

'No, Max you're not getting out of school today.'

I sighed. 'That never crossed my mind.'

Grandma started to laugh.

'I love you, Grandma.'

'You too, Max.'

I was happy knowing that Grandma was laughing. I went into school with a nice smile on my face.

Daisy

❧

aisy couldn't rest when she got home, so she went
straight round to the gardener's house and knocked
on the door. Much to her surprise, the gardener opened
the door. Most of the time, he wouldn't answer the door.
He was a very secret man living a very secret life, that's
how everybody in the village would describe the gardener.
As the door opened, he greeted Daisy with a smile.

'Hello, Daisy! How may I help you?' he asked.

Daisy didn't know where to start. She stood there in
silence for a moment, then she said, 'May I speak with
you?'

The gardener looked a bit startled. 'Yes, yes, of course
you may speak to me. How can I help you, Daisy?'

Daisy was now slightly shocked at herself and started to
wonder what she was doing. The gardener had never
bothered anybody, she thought, and yet he has helped
everybody in the village one way or the other. She realised
that the gardener had never made small talk with anybody,
and yet everybody talked about him. The gardener had
never asked for anything from anybody, and yet he had
given so much without reward. She was standing there,
with a man she'd known for many, many years ... and she
couldn't get even one word out of her mouth. Daisy just
stood there, looking at this very old man who had the
kindest smile she'd ever seen.

She muttered something, but it came out as a small croak, and the gardener asked if she was well.

'Yes, yes, I'm fine. I just, ah well, oh dear, what was I thinking?'

The old man was looking very puzzled, so much so that he stepped out of his house and took a look around, he then said to Daisy, 'Let me help you.'

'Okay, yes,' she muttered, regretting not just minding her own business.

The gardener said, 'Are you sure you're okay?'

Daisy looked straight at him, nodding her head.

He seemed concerned for her, because he tried to make small talk. 'I remember your Jim,' he said, 'and I remember when you and Jim were living in that house, the one that your Tom lives in now, with his, family.'

Daisy felt her anxiety lessen a little, and she found herself able to answer this time. 'Yes, we loved every minute of our time together in that house, in this village. I wouldn't change a thing.' Then Daisy paused and started to think of the real reason why she had decided to come and speak to the gardener. She was in a daze again and couldn't help but think of those two little lost children.

The gardener looked at Daisy straight in the eyes and said with a stern voice, 'Daisy, LET'S GET TO POINT OF YOUR VISIT! I CAN CLEARLY SEE YOU HAVE SOMETHING ON YOUR MIND.'

'Yes, yes, of course. I've come to see you because I wanted to ask you ...' I paused again slightly ... 'were the two little children that got lost through the secret gate your children?' There. She'd got the words out. That wasn't so bad. But then she saw the look on the gardener's face – now five shades lighter, and his eyes were full of sorrow. 'I'm really sorry,' she added, then paused again, because she wanted to say his name but didn't know it. How could she stand there and ask the gardener questions and not have the good manners to find out his name first? She felt ridiculous, and once again wished she had minded her own business.

The gardener looked at Daisy and, just like that, he said, 'Winston is my name.'

Daisy could see that he was very disappointed with her.

'Have I ever asked anything of you, Daisy?' he continued.

Daisy felt sick. No words would come.

Winston put his head down and walked back into the house, shutting the door behind him.

This was no less than she deserved, Daisy thought. She'd lived in this village for many years, and all the while, the gardener was there he had even helped to look after her garden from time to time, and in all those years she hadn't even bothered to ask the gardener his name. Daisy felt a deep shame. And then she felt the determination to make it up to Winston – there, she knew his name now, and a fine name it was. Winston.

Daisy returned to the house feeling angry, confused and guilty, though guilty of exactly what she wasn't sure. She phoned Naga and Fred to cancel their visit, telling them she had an appointment which she had forgotten about. This was not true, but she wanted time to think about this situation. Max was a very clever young man – however, Daisy didn't think he realised the significance of what he had said. Now everything had fallen into place for Daisy, and she wasn't about to let this go until she had all the answers.

She decided to go over to the shop and speak to Mr and Mrs Fudge. Above everybody else in the village, Mr and Mrs Fudge had spent the most time with Winston, so she would see if they had anything to add to her idea. As Daisy arrived at the shop, the couple were quite busy serving customers, so she waited for a while. They could see that Daisy wanted to talk to them, so after everybody had left the shop, Mrs Fudge said, 'Daisy, come into the back room and I will make you a cup of tea.'

Daisy sat down.

Mrs Fudge asked, 'Is everything okay?'

'I'm not sure, to be honest, May. I will get straight to the point. Last night, young Max came up with the idea that the children who got lost through the secret gate could be the gardener's – I mean Winston's.' May instantly had a smile on her face when Daisy said the gardener's name. 'What are your thoughts on that theory? Do you think the children could have been Winston's children?'

May looked shocked. 'I've never considered that, if I'm honest.'

'Well, I've been awake all night, and after taking the children to school, I went round to see the gardener – I mean Winston – to ask him if the missing children were his, and Winston just shut the door in my face, so I believe I'm onto something.'

'You know that Winston is a very secret man, and he doesn't like any fuss?'

'Yes, yes, I understand all that, but what are your thoughts on the missing children?'

'I'm really sorry, Daisy, but I can't shed any light on your theory.'

'I just wanted to ask because you have had the most involvement with the gardener – I mean Winston.'

'You are right, but in all the years we have been dealing with him, I still have no idea how old he is, if he has ever been married.'

41

'Well, I have made a decision, May,' Daisy said decisively.

May looked at Daisy. 'What do you mean?'

'I'm going to Horsey Gap to see the witch in her alcazar.'

May looked horrified. 'Do you think that's a good idea, Daisy?'

'Not really, but I don't feel I have any choice.'

With that, Mr Fudge walked into the back room. It appeared he'd heard at least some of their conversation. 'There is always a choice, Daisy. You know that Winston is a secret man who likes to live a secret life. I don't think he will appreciate what you are saying or what you are planning to do.'

Daisy replied, 'I know you're right, John but I think after everything he's done for this village, we owe it to him. What if I'm right? And we could, after everything he's done for all of us, reunite Winston with his children. And then there is the question of his wife – what happened to her? Do any of us know?' Daisy could feel herself getting angry about how little she knew, how little anyone knew.

Mr and Mrs Fudge nodded.

'You're right, Daisy,' John said. 'Because Winston is so unselfish, we have just left him to get on with things. Now, if you're planning to go to Horsey Gap and see the witch in her alcazar, there a few things you need to know. One: Horsey Gap is roughly twenty-five miles from here, and after the first five miles, the terrain changes very dramatically after every five miles.'

May looked at her husband. 'How do you know?' she asked him.

'Because then the gardener got hurt all those years ago. It was me who told the witch.'

42

May was starting to look very confused. 'But I don't understand. How did you know that Winston had been hurt?'

'Because he never made his delivery to the shop, and in all the years he has delivered to this shop, have you ever known him to be late?'

'No, never,' said Mrs Fudge.

'Exactly,' said Mr Fudge. 'And like you, Daisy, I followed my instinct and made the journey. It was very hard, but I made it. So, make sure you take your time, drive very steady and be prepared for anything. And I mean anything, from a marching band to a desert storm. Anything can happen, so you must stay focused, and you will get through. Once you start the second part of the journey, you cannot turn back. Are you taking the children?'

Daisy didn't hesitate. 'Yes, the children are totally fascinated by the garden and the witch, and if I leave them, I imagine they would very upset.'

'Well, take it from me, Daisy,' Mr Fudge said, 'it's no easy task to get to Horsey Gap.'

Mrs Fudge said, 'The children can stay with us if you like.'

'Thank you very much, but I can't leave them.'

'Another thing,' said Mr Fudge. 'I think your theory could be right.'

Mrs Fudge had tears in her eyes. 'I don't think you should go, Daisy.'

'I understand what you're saying, May, but in this case, I feel I have no choice. The gardener – Winston – has been so kind to all of us for many, many years, and if I don't make this journey to ask the witch directly, I fear that I will have to live the rest of my life with regrets. Tell me, Mr Fudge, was the witch nice?'

'Yes, she is nice, but very stern, and she treats visitors suspiciously, so you will have to make sure the witch understands that your visit is purely for your concern for Winston. The witch will do anything to help him. Oh, and one other thing – never speak to the witch until she speaks to you. Wait until she has finished speaking. Never interrupt her, and make sure you follow her exact instructions. Oh, and look, but never touch.'

Okay, thank you both for your advice. Once I have collected the children, we're leaving straight away so we can be home before dark.'

'Good idea,' said Mr Fudge, 'and stick to that plan. Don't allow yourself to be carried away by the things you see and hear. Stick to the plan.'

Daisy nodded. 'Just one more thing before I go.'

'Yes?' said Mr Fudge.

'Can you write down the directions to Horsey Gap?'

'I'll print you off a map.'

'That would be very helpful,' said Daisy.

Mr Fudge went to the front of the shop to print off the map for Daisy, and soon he returned and handed it over. 'Before you go,' he said, 'I'm just going to run your car around to the garage and check the tyre pressures, water, oil and fill your car with fuel.'

'Oh goodness, John, that's very kind of you. If you're sure it's no bother.'

'No problem. Just give twenty minutes.'

Just then, a few customers entered the shop. They looked around.

'Everything okay, Mrs Fudge?' one asked.

'Yes, thank you.'

'No Mr Fudge today?'

'Oh, yes, he's here, but he's just popped out for

something.' Then Mrs Fudge looked over to Daisy.

'Well, to be honest,' Daisy said, 'Mr Fudge has taken my car over to the garage.'

The customer was looking very confused. 'Has your car gone wrong, Daisy?'

Daisy hesitated for a moment but quickly thought it was best to tell them where she was going in case anything went wrong. 'As it happens, I'm going to visit the witch at Horsey Gap, in her alcazar,' she said calmly.

A look of horror appeared on all of the customers' faces. 'Do you think that's wise?'

'Not really, but it's something I need to do. You could say like it's on my bucket list, and I've promised the children.'

'That's a pretty big promise, Daisy,' replied, one of the customers. 'Rather you than me.'

Trying not to look too nervous, Daisy replied, 'Well, a promise is a promise.'

Just then, Fred walked into the shop, 'Hello, Daisy. How did your appointment go?'

Daisy faltered. She had forgotten that she'd told Fred she had an appointment. 'Fred, I never had an appointment, and I'm sorry for lying, but I needed to see the gardener. Did you know the gardener's name is Winston?'

'No,' replied Fred. 'How have you found that out?'

'He told me.'

'So, you never had an appointment today?'

'No. Sorry.'

'Okay, no worries. I had plenty to catch up with today.'

Just then, Mr Fudge returned. He walked over to Daisy and handed back her keys.

'You're all set, Daisy. I've checked everything, even filled up your screen washers.'

'Are you going somewhere, Daisy?' asked Fred.

'Yes. I'm going to Horsey Gap to visit the witch, in her alcazar.'

Fred also looked shocked. 'Whatever for, may I ask?'

'It's a long story, and I'm already late to collect the children from school.'

'Yes, of course,' said Fred. 'But I think I'd better come with you, Daisy.'

Daisy could see the sense in this. 'Are you sure, Fred?'

'Yes. I'm not letting you go on your own, with children. Your Jim would never forgive me.'

Daisy saw that Mr and Mrs Fudge had a look of relief on the faces.

'Okay, but I'm leaving now. Once I've collected the children, we are going straight from school.'

'Okay, no problem. Ready when you are,' said Fred.

'Let's go.'

Daisy knew she was onto something, and she thought that she owed it to Winston to find out the truth and ask the witch if there was any way of reuniting Winston with the children. She also knew that the journey was not going to be easy, and Daisy wouldn't say it, but she was afraid.

Fred asked Daisy, 'Why are we going to Horsey Gap?'

'Because young Max said something last night, and it has made realise that just because a person never makes any trouble and has never asked anything of anybody and is always prepared to go the extra mile for anybody that crosses their path, doesn't mean that they themselves don't need help or support from time to time. We've all taken him for granted. The gardener, who I now know as Winston, may need some help, so, just like he has always done his best for our village without reward, I'm going to do my best for him.'

Fred sat in silence, listening, and then finally he said, 'What is your point, Daisy?'

'It is my belief that the two children that got lost through the secret gate within the walled garden are Winston's children.'

'What makes you believe that, Daisy?'

'Think about it, Fred. Winston very rarely leaves the walled garden. He is in there most days from dawn till dusk. And when he goes off with his caravan, the witch watches over the garden until he returns. And another thing – we have lived in the village for many years, but has anybody ever remembered the missing children or mentioned whose children they were?'

Fred was silent and seemed in deep thought. The pair sat in silence while Daisy drove to the school. After a few minutes, he finally replied, 'You have got a point, Daisy, and I understand your reasons. I cannot remember anybody ever telling me who the children's parents were. What do you think the witch can do though?'

Daisy quickly replied, 'I don't know until I ask her, but one thing I'm sure of is I will never rest again unless I make this journey and ask that question.'

'Okay, fair enough. But how are you going to tell the children?'

'They're enthralled and fascinated by the walled garden and really want to visit it, so I'll explain that we are going to ask the witch if we can enter the walled garden. However, Max has already worked out that the lost children could be Winston's children. Do you know, Fred, that I am really pleased with myself that I now know the gardener by his name, and what a fine name he has – Winston. Anyway, getting back to Kelvin, Yazz and Max, I'm hoping they'll be so excited that we are going to

Horsey Gap to see the witch in her alcazar that they won't take too much notice of my real reason.'

'Okay,' said Fred. 'Let's keep our fingers crossed.'

'One more thing before the kids get in the car,' Daisy said. 'Remember Kelvin is autistic and doesn't like any change.'

'I understand,' said Fred.

As they arrived at the school, the children had just walked out.

Max

≈

'Perfect timing, Grandma!' I said as I got in, nodding a hello to Fred.

Kelvin was just looking at the car but making no attempt to get in, and Daisy knew straight away what was wrong, so she got out of the car and said, 'It's okay, Kelvin. Uncle Fred is coming with us.' Kelvin was looking very confused, so Daisy went on. 'You know how last night I got very upset? Well, I've decided today that we are all going to see the witch at Horsey Gap in her alcazar to ask her if we can visit the walled garden.'

Kelvin looked at Daisy and said, 'That's a good idea.'

Whilst Grandma was explaining to Kelvin, I mentioned to Uncle Fred that Kelvin always sits in the front, even in Dad's car.

Uncle Fred said, 'Ah, yes, of course, I remember now.'

Fred quickly hopped out the passenger door and jumped in the back with me and Yazz. By this time, Daisy had finished explaining to Kelvin, who looked relieved to discover that the front seat was now empty.

'Grandma, what's going on?' asked Yazz.

'I've decided to go to Horsey Gap to see the witch in her alcazar and ask her straightforward if we can visit the garden.'

I gasped. 'Wow, that's a big decision. Are we going straight there?'

'Yes.'

'What, leaving right now?'

'It's precisely 15.35, which means in Toronto, Canada, it's approximately 10.35,' Kelvin chimed in.

'Bravo, Kelvin!' Fred shouted. 'Super timekeeping.'

Kelvin had a big smile on his face.

Grandma looked relieved. Kelvin speaking up was a sign that Kelvin would be okay with Uncle Fred. Grandma turned around and looked at me and Yazz. 'We are going to Horsey Gap to ask the witch about visiting the walled garden.'

'I need to ask about the children who went through the secret gate,' I said.

'I'll do all the talking, Max,' she said, in a tone I knew not to argue with.

I sighed and said, 'Okay, you're in charge, Grandma.'

'That's correct, Max.'

I felt so excited.

Grandma said, 'This won't be an easy mission, so I must prepare you three for what is come. Horsey Gap is roughly 25 miles from here. The first five miles is normal road, and then the next twenty miles will be very unusual, judging by what Mr Fudge has told me, so please keep your eyes open at all times and let me know if you see anything that you think I must know about.'

'What do you mean?' I asked.

'I'm not sure, Max, but I think you will see what I mean when you see it happen.'

Yazz asked, 'Grandma, do you think this is the right thing to do?'

'Yes, of course. We must always search for the truth, no matter how hard that journey may be. The gardener has been very loyal to the village and always done his best for everybody who lives there, maintaining the garden keeping the shop full of the finest produce and looking after everybody else's gardens whenever he has spare time.'

'He is quite incredible,' said Kelvin.

'I agree,' said Fred.

I couldn't contain myself at that moment. 'Horsey Gap here we come!' I shouted. 'Grandma, didn't I tell you that I was going to see the witch?'

'Yes you did, Max.'

'I also know that the witch is going to really like me.'

'And what makes you think that the witch is going to like you?'

'Well, because I'm nice.'

'And who told you that?' said Fred.

'Myself. Yes, I told myself that I was very nice.'

Uncle Fred was laughing to himself.

Yazz eyed Grandma, who was looking at a map. 'Do you know the route?'

'I will do, once I've studied this map.'

'Why don't you use your sat nav?'

'Technology will not get us to Horsey Gap, Yazz. I will need a good sense of direction. Now, fasten your seatbelts. Remember to keep your eyes open at all times.'

Fred suggested that Grandma give him the map so he could be co-pilot, and then thankfully Kelvin suggested that Uncle Fred sit in the front of the car.

'Well done, Kelvin. That's a good idea,' said Grandma.

With Uncle Fred now sat in the front of the car, we were finally ready to leave.

We left the school on the usual route, and when we got to the sharp corner, there was a sharp left-hand turn that I'd never noticed before. As Grandma made the turn, I noticed the name of the road: Horsey Road. 'This is Horsey Road!' I shouted.

'Well spotted, Max. Good to know we're on the right road,' said Grandma.

I starting to sing a little song: 'We're going to Horsey Gap! We're going to Horsey Gap!'

Then everybody joined in. 'We're going to Horsey Gap!'

The first few miles were pretty normal. 'Grandma,' I said, 'You said we must keep our eyes open.'

'Yes, Max.'

'What exactly are we looking for?'

'Well, that's it, Max. I don't know. I'm hoping we will spot it first.'

Uncle Fred was watching the road very carefully, and just like a co-pilot he was explaining every inch of the road ahead: 'Left bend coming up ... Righthand bend coming up ... Bridge ... Traffic light five hundred yards ahead.' I thought to myself that it was a good job Fred had come because Yazz and I wouldn't have been able to cope with being co-pilot, and although Kelvin would have understood the map better, he would have got stressed under the pressure.

After about four miles we came to a fork in the road. We stopped.

'Which way?' Grandma asked.

'Judging by this map ... well, this fork in the road simply isn't on the map,' Fred muttered.

'Okay. What now?' said Grandma.

We all paused for a moment, the sound of the engine the only noise.

'Oh, look!' said Fred, sounding very relieved. 'There's a signpost on the ground over there.'

'Where? I can't see it,' replied Grandma.

'Just there. Let me get out and have a look.'

Then the door of the car opened, and from out of nowhere a man appeared in the doorway.

The man looked in the car and said, 'Going somewhere nice?'

With a look of shock on her face, Grandma said out loud in a stern tone of voice, 'We hope so.'

'Well, I have to say you look lost to me,' said the man.

Fred had gotten out of the car and was just checking our route. He had the map in his hand and he was looking at the ground where the sign lay.

Kelvin asked Grandma, 'Why have we stopped?' I could tell Kelvin didn't like the man opening the car door.

Grandma replied, 'Once Fred has worked out the route, we shall be on our way.'

Fred came back towards the car, but then he shut the car door while still outside, then smiled pleasantly at the stranger.

I said to Grandma, 'Why don't you just ask the man which way to go?'

'I'm sure Fred will ask him now, Max.'

The two men were chatting amicably, and then they walked over to the broken signpost. I knew Fred was trying to work out which way the sign had been fastened to the post. The man was still chatting away to Fred, but I could see that by now, Fred was not interested in what the man was saying and was just trying very hard to work out which way we needed to go.

Grandma turned to look at us and I saw she was getting impatient. 'Okay, you all sit here. I'm just going to try and work this out.' Grandma got out of the car and walked over to Fred. We heard her words to him – 'Are you getting anywhere?'

He had the sign in his hand and an anxious look on his face. 'No.'

The man was still chatting, and Grandma looked at him and said, 'Please, sir, can you tell me what are you talking about?'

He replied, 'I was just telling this good man how the signpost got broken.'

'And why would we want to know that?'

'Well, because it's broken.'

I noticed that Kelvin was getting stressed. 'Why are they taking so long?' he asked. 'Fred has been out of the car for exactly eight minutes and forty-five, forty-six, forty-seven, forty-eight—'

'Okay, don't panic, Kelvin. Calm down.'

'I don't like this situation. It's not good. We should leave.'

Yazz patted Kelvin's shoulder. 'We will soon, don't worry.'

Kelvin continued to count.

Yazz continued, 'We are waiting because if the signpost was not broken it would tell us which direction to travel in.'

Kelvin calmed down at this explanation, but he was still counting to himself.

Travelling in Grandma's car is great because it has a panoramic roof view. This means almost the whole roof is glass, so you can look up at the sky. As I looked up, I saw a crow circling, and I watched it lazily. After a while, the crow glided down and perched itself on a fence near the car. If I hadn't known better, I'd have thought the crow was listening. It turned its head towards me and I noticed it had green eyes. I blinked hard, then as I turned to Yazz to tell her about it, the bird flew away. I knew better than to try to tell Yazz about a green-eyed bird when she couldn't see it with her own eyes.

I could hear Grandma saying, 'Well that's one thing we can agree on – the signpost is broken. Thanks for the info.'

Clearly failing to pick up on Grandma's sarcasm, the man nodded his head cheerily. 'You're welcome! I'm happy to help.'

'That's great, so tell me, which way do we need to go to get to Horsey Gap?'

'Ahh, you should have said that in the first place! I would have told you!' said the man.

Grandma was looking so angry by that point. 'So, please, sir, which way is it to Horsey Gap?'

The man looked straight at Grandma, took a deep breath, and said, 'Let me introduce myself first.'

'Do you have to?' said Grandma, her face reddening, her voice growing sharp. 'Only we have to keep moving and we've already lost ten minutes.'

'Time is all we have,' said the man. 'Make the most of every second. Now, don't you want to know my name?'

'It doesn't sound like we have any choice in the matter. Do tell.'

'Well, it's not going to take me more than a few seconds to tell you my name.'

Grandma was completely out of patience by now. 'Yes, yes. Please, sir, tell me your name.'

Again he took a deep breath. 'It's a long story—'

'No. No, it's not, because we are leaving, right now,' Grandma snapped.

'But ... you don't know which way to go!'

'Yes I do,' said Grandma. She picked up the sign and held it up to the post. 'Look, Fred, That's the way the sign was fitted to the post. If you look carefully, you can see the paint marks, so that means the signpost was facing in that direction.'

Fred's eyes lit up. 'Ah! Daisy, you're right! Well done. Come on, let's go.'

The man looked at Grandma and Fred and said, 'Are you leaving?'

Grandma turned around and replied, dead serious, 'No, sir. We are staying for tea. Put the kettle on.'

'I don't have a kettle,' replied the man, 'but I have got some advice for you.'

'Oh you do, do you?' chuckled Grandma, rolling her eyes. 'And what might that be?'

'Don't talk to strangers,' said the man. And on the next part of your journey, there will be an elephant.'

Grandma, who I swear had steam coming from her ears now, quickly replied, 'Don't tell me, it's white.'

'No, don't be ridiculous,' said the man. 'It's pink.'

Fred couldn't stop laughing, and I found myself wanting to join in, what with Grandma being so impatient and the man trying to tell us his life story.

'And whatever you do,' the man continued, 'don't try and overtake. You must follow the elephant. And just in case we never meet again, my name is Ralph. And if we do meet again, it's still Ralph.' Then the nicest smile appeared on Ralph's face. He had a look of kindness that I had never seen before.

'Goodbye Ralph. We certainly won't forget you,' Grandma said, her voice softening a little.

A big smile appeared on Ralph's face as if he'd just had his greatest achievement.

As Grandma drove off at speed, we waved to Ralph from the back window, as if we'd known him our whole lives. I wondered at how someone could have such an impact in just about ten minutes.

'I like Ralph,' said Kelvin.

'And me,' said Yazz.

Grandma finally said, 'Yes, I suppose he was nice, and I'm sorry for being in such a hurry. Ralph must think I'm terrible.'

'No he wouldn't,' said Fred.

'It's just part of being older, I think. I can't help it.'

'Oh Grandma,' I said, reaching forward to pat her arm.

'We don't care,' said Yazz. 'We love, even if you are very inpatient at times.'

We were back on track with our journey. Yazz asked Grandma, 'Why did you say to Ralph that you think the elephant's white?'

'It's a saying. Ever since people have been designing and making things – and when I say things, I mean everything from bridges to buildings, from cars to boats – sometimes someone comes up with the most amazing idea and spends vast amounts of money time and effort, but for some reason, the idea just doesn't work. Maybe, for one reason or another, people just don't take to the idea or item. When that happens, people call the idea a white elephant.'

I replied, 'So, it could be that something has gone wrong?'

'Yes, something like that.'

The road was getting very bumpy and narrow. 'Okay, you three. Keep your eyes open for a pink elephant,' said Grandma.

I asked, 'Grandma, do you think we are really going to see a pink elephant?'

Kelvin said, 'I would love to see an elephant of any colour.'

In the distance I could see a bridge – a suspension bridge to be exact – and I could see it moving from side to side. 'Look, Grandma! There is a bridge.'

'Yes, and we are heading straight for it.'

Within five minutes we were going over the bridge. It was very tall, and it seemed like we were driving up to it forever.

Grandma said, 'I don't like this bridge.'

'It's moving,' Fred replied. 'All suspension bridges move in the wind. I will be happier once we reach the other side.' Fred returned his attention to the map. 'Blimey. This bridge is two miles long.'

We finally reached the other side. I could see a look of relief on Grandma's face. Once over the other side, it was as if we had just landed in a different country. We all turned to look back and we could only see the bridge, nothing beyond it. The sun was just setting.

Kelvin said, 'Grandma, we are in Tanzania. This is the Serengeti. The time here is just after 6 p.m.'

'Well done, Kelvin. I was beginning to worry about where we were,' said Grandma. 'Mr Fudge did say to be prepared for anything, but not in my wildest dreams could I have imagined this.'

Everybody in the car was silently looking around in amazement. We couldn't believe where we were – it was just so beautiful.

'I've always wanted to go on safari,' said Fred. 'My dad told me if you live long enough you will live to see everything. I feel like a kid going to the zoo for the first time.'

As I looked out, I could see giraffes on the horizon, and zebras too. 'This is the best place I've ever been,' I said. 'Thank you, Grandma and Fred, for bringing us here.'

'You're very welcome, Max.' Grandma had slowed the car down so we could take in our surroundings.

'We'd best keep moving, Daisy,' Fred said, 'because as well has the beautiful giraffes and zebras there are also lions and tigers, and as much as I would love to see them, they will be much happier to see us.'

'Yes, you're right, Fred. I hadn't thought of that.' With that, Grandma made the car pick up speed.

A bit further down the road, it got very bumpy, so we needed to slow down again. And then, as Fred had suggested, there they were: loins. A complete pride, in fact. I counted them – fifteen of them. They were magnificent and full of life. As our car moved towards them, the lions started to get curious and moved towards us. This was fast becoming a very dangerous place. I could sense that Grandma and Fred were also slightly afraid.

Grandma said, 'Okay, you three. I know we are in the car, and that the car is moving, but please sit very still and do not make any eye contact with the lions.' I don't know why, but I started to laugh. Grandma was holding on to the steering wheel so tight that her knuckles were white. 'Max, please be quiet.'

'Sorry.'

Just then, we could hear a loud thundering noise and the ground was rumbling. Yazz started to scream as Grandma turned around to calm her down, and I saw that not only were her knuckles white, but now so was her face, and she had an expression of horror. I quickly turned my head to see what Grandma was looking at because it was obvious to me something was coming up behind us. Kelvin started to count again, and this time it was '1 p.m., 2 p.m., 3 p.m., 4 p.m. ....'

I told him to stay calm, and Kelvin nodded.

Fred shouted, 'Keep driving, Daisy!'

As I looked, I could see a herd of elephants running towards the car.

Kelvin was holding his hand over his ears, and I put my arms around him to help keep him calm. 'Kelvin, look at those beautiful trees,' I said, at the same time trying very hard to keep myself calm.

Grandma quickly turned her attention to driving again. The elephants were all around us by then, running very fast past us. I noticed that the lions seemed to be afraid of the elephants. This was a relief but also still very scary, because the elephants were very large. Then again, I knew the elephants would not harm us providing we never got too close or in their way. As well as feeling scared, I also felt very excited. The elephants seemed much bigger than any elephants I'd seen in the zoo. One by one the elephants thundered past the car, and the very last elephant was a baby, which was slightly pink in colour.

I shouted out, 'Grandma! Look, Grandma! There's Ralph's elephant – the pink one! As I was telling Grandma, I couldn't take my eyes off the little pink elephant.

'Remember what Ralph said?' Fred said to Grandma.

Grandma nodded. 'I shouldn't overtake the pink elephant.'

And so we followed the little elephant. I noticed that the lions had moved on – in fact, they had moved on so far that I couldn't see them any more. I guessed that the elephants thundering past us had encouraged the lions to move away. All our fear had gone now. Kelvin had a look of relief on his face, and thankfully Yazz had stopped screaming. We were now just following the little pink elephant, who was following the big grey elephants. We were like a convoy! Grandma's car fitted in very well with the elephants because it was also grey. As Ralph had instructed, we followed the pink elephant, Grandma staying back, not too close in case the little pink elephant was afraid of the car.

Looking out the window, I could see a lake and in the lake was there were rhinos. 'Kelvin! Yazz! Look at the rhinos!' I shouted. They were massive – we'd never seen a real rhino before.

After following the elephants for about two miles, we came to a river, and Grandma and Fred looked horrified. 'How are we going to get across the river?' said Grandma.

They were both looking around, still following the little pink elephant.

That's when I first wished I'd never mentioned going to see the witch, because this journey was clearly too much for Grandma, and I know Mum and Dad wouldn't be best pleased with Grandma taking us three all the way. I looked up and to see a black crow circling again – but surely that couldn't be the same crow I'd seen earlier.

Just then, Yazz shouted out, 'Look! There is a little boat – a ferry! See, I knew I could see something.' I looked and saw the elephants all walking towards the little ferry. I decided once again to keep my mouth shut about the crow. Nobody would believe that a crow was following us anyway. As we approached the water's edge, the elephants all started to walk into the river and surround the little boat. Then they stopped and turned around, all except the little pink one looking at us. As we got closer I spotted a man on the little boat. I watched as he dropped down the gangplank so that we could drive aboard, still following the little elephant onto the boat. Once we were on board, all the big elephants started to tug the little boat across the river.

61

So this was why we needed to follow the pink elephant. It was a good job we'd met Ralph.

Kelvin said, 'Ralph was very helpful, Grandma.'

'Yes, he was,' she replied.

As the little boat started to move slowly across the river, the captain walked over to the car, and Grandma put down her window.

'Hello,' said the captain.

Grandma replied, 'Hello.'

I looked up at the captain and smiled, and he smiled back. He said, 'Are you enjoying the journey, children?' As he spoke, he sounded just like Ralph, and when he smiled he looked just like Ralph, and for a split second, I thought it was Ralph. I was just about to say, 'Hello, Ralph' when the captain said, 'My name is Ralph.'

I shouted out loud, 'I knew you were Ralph!'

Ralph looked straight at me and that big smile appeared on his face again, with the same look as last time Ralph – that look of achievement.

Grandma and Fred looked a bit shocked and seemed lost for words, especially Grandma after she had been so impatient with Ralph. But Ralph didn't seem worried – he was just glad to see us all again.

I said, 'We followed your instructions, Ralph. Thank you very much.'

With that, Grandma said, 'Yes, yes, good job you told us to follow the pink elephant.'

Ralph smiled and said, 'You're welcome.'

Grandma said to Ralph, 'I owe you an apology.'

Ralph replied, 'You owe me nothing. I could see you were in a rush, and I was holding you back. You did the right thing, because if you had spent any more time chatting to me, you would have missed this ferry crossing, and I was only chatting about nothing anyway.'

Daisy replied, 'Well, thank you for your help.'

'It's no trouble. As I said before, I'm happy to help.' Then Ralph told us about the next part of the journey. 'It will be very hot. Don't stop for anything. Keep moving, but no faster than 50mph so as the tyres on your car don't get too hot.' Ralph then handed Fred five large bottles of water. 'Now, remember, no stopping.'

By then the elephants had managed to reach the other side of the river. Ralph dropped the gangplank and the pink elephant left the boat and returned to his herd, and we went on our way. Yazz, Kelvin and I turned around to wave goodbye to Ralph as we had done the time before, and Ralph had that big smile on his face again as he waved back to us. I really wanted Ralph to come with us, but this was not possible because we only had five seats and they were all taken.

As we started on the third leg of the journey, we could all feel the heat straight away – Ralph had been right. Grandma needed to put the air conditioning full on.

Fred asked Kelvin, 'Where are we?'

Kelvin looked at the sky. He replied, 'Australia. That's why it's so hot, and lucky for us it's most probably the coolest time of the day to travel. He looked at the dashboard clock. '16.07, and Australia is roughly eight and a half hours in front of us, so the time here is 00.37.'

I noticed that although the night sky looked darker than I had ever seen it before, the moon was very bright, and the sky very clear. The area seemed to be a vast, wide-open space, and space was just how the sky looked – we felt like we were driving on the moon. I had never seen the sky look so beautiful. I could see what looked to me like the cosmos. The car was completely silent again. We were all looking in amazement at the sky. Because the space was so open and so vast, you could see hundreds of shooting stars, as if they were raining down on us. It was awesome.

Then Kelvin seemed to notice something in the distance, and I looked too. I saw a large shadow, which looked like the outline of a mountain.

Grandma noticed us looking, and looked too. 'Well spotted,' said Grandma. It looked like the road was heading straight for it. We then all focused our attention back on the sky. I had never realised just how many colours the sky at night could display. Grandma was only driving slowly, and we were all taking everything in. We had never seen so much sky at once.

As we got nearer to the shadow of the mountain, Yazz shouted out, 'I know what that shadow of a mountain is!'

We went quiet to listen to Yazz.

'It's Uluru, formerly known as Ayers Rock,' she told us proudly.

Fred and Grandma were so excited they couldn't get their words out.

'What did you say? Are you sure, Yazz?' asked Grandma.

'Yes, Grandma. It makes sense. We are in Australia, isn't that right, Kelvin?'

'According to my timing, yes, and this wide-open space – nothing that we can see for miles.'

Fred said, 'Yazz, I think you could be right.'

I could hear the excitement in Fred's voice.

Kelvin was also excited. 'This journey is amazing!' he exclaimed. 'We don't know what's coming next.'

Then all of a sudden, the sky seemed to darken, and the temperature dropped. We noticed this because Grandma needed to turn off the air conditioning. And then came the rain. At first, it was only light rain, and then it got heavier and heavier, and then we could hear the rolling thunder. After this came, the lightning lit up the sky like nothing I'd ever seen before. It felt like the world was coming to an end. Kelvin was very afraid and he started to counting again, so Yazz and I wrapped our arms around him and calmed him down. 'Don't worry, Kelvin,' I said. 'It will soon be over.'

The atmosphere in the car had changed from excitement to fear. Yazz and I were both very scared but we tried not to show it for the benefit of Kelvin. Grandma had slowed the car down and the windscreen wipers seemed like they were going so fast that they would fall off. The lightning was amazing – it was lighting up the sky for miles. This was probably the best place on earth to see lightning.

We finally got to Uluru. We could only see the outline most of the time, but when the lightning flashed it illuminated it, and it looked magnificent.

'Take a good look, kids,' said Grandma, 'because I'm not coming back.'

After we got past the rock, it was as if our journey in Australia was over. The rain had stopped, the lightning had gone, and the sun was starting to rise ... and up ahead was another bridge.

The bridge was very old. I could see it had big steel arches.

Fred said, 'That looks like the Sydney Harbour Bridge.'

'I think I've visited that bridge before,' said Kelvin.

Grandma replied, 'No, Kelvin, you've seen the Tyne Bridge before.'

Fred said, 'Actually, the Sydney Harbour Bridge was built by the same company – a firm called Dorman Long of

Middlesbrough. They based the design on their 1928 Tyne Bridge. The Sydney Harbour Bridge opened around 1932.' Uncle Fred sure knew his history when it came to bridges. 'So, both Tyne Bridge and Sydney Harbour Bridge are made by the same company and look the same. So, Kelvin and Daisy, you're both right.'

We started to travel over the bridge, then once we reached the other side, there was a large set of gates, which were closed. As we got nearer I could make out a crow, sat on the left gate post. It seemed to be watching us intently.

'Wait, is that a gatekeeper?' Kelvin said.

'Well spotted,' said Grandma.

We pulled up, and the gatekeeper started to open the gates. Grandma put her window down and thanked the gatekeeper.

He put his head down to the window and asked, 'Where are you going?'

Grandma replied, 'Horsey Gap.'

'It's been a long time since anybody passed through here to go to Horsey Gap,' he replied. The gatekeeper was dressed in what looked like a military uniform, with lots of medals on the chest. The uniform was navy blue, decorated with lots of gold braiding. He looked very important, and when he spoke he had a very clear, stern, well-spoken voice.

'I have some advice for you, for the next stage of your journey.'

We were all listening very intently, nodding.

'From here, you will travel to a place not yet discovered officially. It is known as Pleasure Island. You can't find the island any other way than through this journey. Now, listen very carefully. Do not stop. Do not get out of your car, no matter how convenient a stop may feel. There lives a very greedy old man who owns most of the island, all except one shop. He will try to make you spend money – all your money, in fact. Before he arrived on Pleasure Island many years ago, it was a very precious place, and all the little shops, restaurants, bars, cafes and amusement were very profitable businesses, and everybody who lived and worked on the island loved being there. And then, when the greedy old man arrived on the island he brought the pleasure park, positioned it in the centre of the island, and like all the rest of the businesses it was a very profitable business. The island was a very beautiful place, and thousands and thousands of people from everywhere would visit the island all year round. The island had the most beautiful beaches and amazing views and an excellent promenade. But once the old man arrived, he was not happy with just organising and running the pleasure park. He wanted everything else on the island – all the shops, bars, cafes, restaurants. Pleasure Island soon became very run down and unsafe. The greedy old man had filled the pleasure park with lots of old broken-down rides and attractions that were unsafe to use, and soon all the visitors stopped visiting Pleasure Island. The greedy old man was very happy because he started to buy up the rest of the businesses on the island. One by one, everybody and every business left the island, all except one – the rock shop. Up to now, this shop has managed to serve the greedy old man.'

Yazz asked, 'Will the old man be at the island today?'

'Yes. He is there every day. He doesn't leave in case he misses a customer.'

Yazz started to laugh. 'What, even Christmas Day?' she asked.

'Yes, even Christmas Day. The greedy old man has taken all the sand off the beach too.'

'Why would he do that?' I asked.

'Because he wanted everybody to spend their money, and not sit on the beach.'

Grandma said, 'I don't like the sound of him.'

The soldier replied, 'He is a terrible man, so remember what I've told you. Don't get out of your car. You may feel like it's okay to stop, because he will be very convincing – but DON'T STOP. If you do, it could be fatal.'

Grandma and Fred thanked the soldier and we left. As we drove away, I noticed a crow. But surely that green-eyed crow hadn't flown all that way. Surely it couldn't be the same crow. As we drove on, I waved goodbye to the soldier. Once again, I wanted the soldier to come with us. He seemed to have a familiar presence about him, almost as if I knew him.

'That soldier reminds me of Dad,' Yazz said thoughtfully.

I replied, 'Yes, I felt like I knew him.'

Yazz and I turned around to see if we could still see the soldier, but he was gone.

Kelvin said, 'I'm missing Mum.'

I felt the same, and I was missing home too. Although we had only been in the car for just over an hour, it felt much longer than that because we had seen so much. Grandma reminded Kelvin that Mum and Dad were only away for a few days.

Kelvin smiled and said, 'Oh yes, you're right, Grandma. I'd forgotten.'

After a couple of miles, we could see Pleasure Island, and as we got nearer, we could hear a loud noise, like shouting.

Fred said, 'Whatever is that noise? And where is it coming from?'

As we approached the Island, we could see there was an old man with a microphone, saying, 'Welcome to Pleasure Island! This is the place where memories are made and dreams come true!'

Grandma said, 'That must be the greedy old man.'

As we drove by, he waved at us as if he knew us, and we waved back. It felt very strange and uncomfortable, and we all started to laugh nervously.

'He looked very, very old,' Kelvin said. 'He looks older than you, Grandma.'

We all started laughing again.

'Thank you, Kelvin,' said Grandma.

Sometimes Kelvin is really funny, and he looked very pleased with himself because we were all laughing. As we drove onto the island, we could see that all the sand had gone from the beach. The sea looked very sad without sand. There were just a few old, dirty deckchairs scattered around in the hole where the sand would have been. The deckchairs had big tags saying *For hire. £25 per hour EACH.*

Fred was shocked. 'Twenty-five pounds! Who in their right mind would pay that to sit on a dirty chair?'

Grandma said, 'Those deckchairs don't even look safe to sit on if you ask me.'

Fred agreed.

All the shops, cafes, bars and restaurants looked very dirty, with broken windows, doors hanging off, and rubbish scattered everywhere. Bins were overflowing with rubbish that looked like it had been there forever.

'This place is a sorry sight,' said Grandma.

As we drove past the rock shop, Grandma slowed down. A man and woman were standing outside. They looked like the owners of the shop. Grandma stopped the car to speak to them – they looked so sad. There wasn't anyone else around, so Grandma put the window down.

'Hello, thank you for stopping.' I could see by the look on their faces that they were genuinely grateful that we had stopped. 'Would you like to buy some rock?'

'Oh, yes please,' said Grandma. 'Can we five sticks, please?'

The look of relief on their faces was so immense that it was worth buying the rock just to see some happiness appear. The man said, 'Don't get out of your car – I will bring the rock to you.'

The man quickly went into the shop to get the rock, and the woman said, 'Have you heard about the greedy old man?' When we all nodded, she continued, 'Please don't get out of your car. If he sees you buying rock from our shop, he won't be happy. He might even ask you to leave.' The lady went on, 'He is a terrible man. This island was a beautiful place to live and work on, full of life. Then the greedy old man arrived, and now it's just sad and lonely. We are the last shop on his list, and every day he offers to buy our shop. He once told my husband that he's useless at selling rock, and if we wanted to be millionaires we would need to follow his instructions. "No, thank you," said my husband. "It's not money that makes us happy. Just look at this place – we wouldn't follow you to a gold mine." The ludicrous old fool.'

The man came back, with our rock wrapped in a brown paper bag so no one could see what was in the bag. Grandma paid for the rock and we said our goodbyes. As we left, I could see sadness come over the shopkeepers again, and I felt sad for them too.

We kept moving. We needed to get to the other side of Pleasure Island.

70

Fred asked Kelvin, 'Where are we now?'

Kelvin looked at the sun and the dashboard clock, and we waited for him to speak. But this time Kelvin couldn't work it out. 'This time I can't tell you, but what I can say is this place feels very dangerous, and I don't like it here.'

There was tumbleweed everywhere, rolling around in the breeze, and a very strange smell. Fred told us that the smell was coming from the rubbish. This place had a strange feeling, like we had just entered a scene for a cowboy film. It felt like we were waiting for someone to say, 'TAKE TWO!' or 'THAT'S A WRAP!', but there was no film crew, nor were there any cameras. In fact, there wasn't a person in sight. Then Kelvin started to count, and this time he was also rocking backwards and forwards, and I could tell he was very stressed.

'I really don't like this place. I don't like this place,' he was repeating himself.

Grandma stopped the car.

Yazz shouted out loud, 'Remember what the soldier said – don't get out the car!'

I had never seen Kelvin so stressed.

I could see Grandma and Fred were very concerned for Kelvin. 'I know, Yazz. But I'm afraid we don't have any choice.' Grandma and Fred got Kelvin out of the car, and Grandma told me and Yazz to stay in the car. On second thoughts,' Grandma said, 'I will lock the door while I go calm Kelvin down.'

Don't be long, in case the greedy old man comes,' said Yazz.

Grandma and Fred walked Kelvin along what was left of the promenade to calm him down. Yazz and I sat in the car, looking at the beach with no sand. It looked very strange. There was a big hole where the sand was supposed to be, and that hole was partly filled with rubbish and it looked like they had tried to cover over the rubbish with some kind of green cloth – it was the most terrible mess – and then sat on top of the stinking mess was a giant statue of a gorilla. The gorilla looked very out of place.

Yazz was also looking at the gorilla, and she said, 'Why would you put a fake giant gorilla on the beach?'

I thought for a second and replied, 'Maybe the greedy old man is hoping the gorilla will eat the rubbish.'

Yazz started to laugh. 'Yes, that would be helpful – the gorilla would never be hungry!'

After about ten minutes, Daisy and Fred guided Kelvin back to the car, and just as they were helping Kelvin to get back in the car, out of nowhere we heard terrible singing. It was echoing all over the place! We all turned to look where the singing was coming from and realised the same old man who had waved at us as we arrived on the island was now singing to us. He looked quite strange, and annoying somehow. He was wearing a shirt and tie with joggers, and a hat that looked like a cowboy hat, and crocodile skin shoes. I've never seen such a ridiculous combination of clothing. Kelvin started counting again and getting stressed. Fred turned to walk over to the old man.

Yazz was also panicking. She shouted, 'No, Fred! No, please get back in the car!'

We had all come to realise pretty quickly that this was the greedy old man we'd been warned about.

Fred said to the greedy old man, who was singing down his microphone very nicely, 'Excuse me, sir, please could you be quiet? We have an autistic young lad with us, and your singing is making him panic.'

The greedy old man looked shocked. 'Don't you like my song?' he asked.

Fred turned and looked at him in disgust. 'It's not the song you're singing. We don't know what you are singing because the noise is horrendous.'

The greedy old man said, 'Would you like me to sing a different song?'

Fred said loudly, 'No! We would prefer you to be quiet if possible.' The greedy old man could not understand that Kelvin was autistic and that all Fred was asking him to do was be quiet.

By now Fred was out of patience, so he turned on his heel and made his way back to the car.

Once we all back in the car, the greedy old man started to walk towards us.

Fred said, 'Jesus, what does he want now,' in a quick and angry tone of voice.

Daisy replied, 'We've only been here twenty minutes, and already this greedy old man is getting on my nerves. Now I can see why everybody has left this island. It seems this greedy old man has got a lot to answer for.'

I noticed the black crow with the green eyes was flying over us.

To get to the other side of the island it was clear to us that we needed to drive through the park, and we all hoped that the greedy old man would not stand in our way – but then he appeared as we approached the gate of the park and started walking alongside the car. We noticed there was some type of barrier across the entrance – it wasn't a gate, it looked more like a cattle gate, something you would see on a farm. As we got nearer the entrance of the park, the old man, who was still walking alongside the car, started dancing and waving his hands about while singing. Kelvin, Yazz and I started to laugh at how ridiculous. I got the feeling he was happy because he knew we needed to go through his park.

Grandma was still driving very slowly, and as we got to the entrance, a young lad wearing exactly the same outfit as the greedy old man opened the gate for us. Grandma looked at the young lad and as she did, he knocked on the window of the car and signalled for her to put down the window, and without thinking, she did so.

The scruffy-looking young lad said, 'Hello, welcome to Pleasure Island!' And with that he raised his hands in the air, shaking them, saying, 'This is where memories are made – Pleasure Island! My name is Trendy Trev.'

Inside the car, you could have heard a pin drop. We were speechless with shock. I thought to myself: Is this fellow real, or just acting?

Fred said, 'Jesus Christ, we've found another one.'

The young lad replied, 'Yes, that's correct, I'm Trendy Trev.'

It felt like was part of live comedy. I was half expecting the live audience to start laughing – but there wasn't any live audience.

Then the greedy old man walked over, still holding his microphone, and stood in front of the car so Grandma needed to stop. The greedy old man walked round to the driver's door, and before Daisy could say anything, the greedy old man's eyes landed on the brown paper bag.

'Have you been to the rock shop?' he asked.

'No,' said Grandma, as she put her hand over the paper bag and then knocked it into the back of the car.

The greedy old man replied, 'Looks like you've been to the rock shop to me.'

Grandma, shaking her head, said, 'No, not us. We haven't been to any rock shop, have we, children?'

'No,' I replied to help her out. 'We don't like rock. It's horrible.'

The greedy old man looked very suspiciously at us all, especially me because I was clutching stick of rock in my hand as I'd been eating it. I tried to put it all my mouth at once, but there was just too much.

The man looked at Grandma and then Fred with a stern look and said, 'Good. I'm glad you haven't been to the rock shop. Soon that rock shop will be mine, and I will need a lorry load of rock every day because only I can sell rock. The current owners know nothing about rock. I'm the best rock seller in the world – "King Rock" I'm known as in these parts of the world.'

I thought to myself, King Ludicrousness sounds more fitting. Everything he was saying was going over the loudspeaker – it was just so funny.

Then he said to us, 'Have you come all this way to see me?'

Fred looked over and in a nice tone of voice he said to the greedy old man, 'We haven't come to see anyone. We're just passing through.'

The greedy old man replied, 'But everybody who visits Pleasure Island only comes to see me. I'm famous, you know.'

Grandma started to laugh, and the greedy old man looked surprised, as if he couldn't work out why she was laughing.

Fred said, 'Well, I'm sorry to disappoint you. We haven't come all this way to see you.'

The greedy old man looked at Fred with an evil x eye and said, 'I'm not speaking to you. I'm taking to this beautiful lady.'

Grandma looked amazed and said, 'Are you speaking to me?'

'Yes,' said the greedy old man. I've never seen such beauty. Where have you been all my life?'

Fred was getting very angry with the greedy old man. 'Okay,' he said in a sharp tone of voice, 'we've had enough of your chitchat. Let's go, Daisy.'

The greedy old man replied, 'But you cannot leave without taking a ride on my new rollercoaster. It cost 10 million lollipops, you know.'

'Rollercoaster? Where is your rollercoaster, may I ask?' Fred said.

The greedy old man pointed to a pile of steel, all laid on the ground, and then repeated, 'That cost 10 million pops, you know.'

Grandma said, 'May I ask how are we going to take a ride on that? It's not even made.'

'It will be today.'

Yazz, Kelvin and I couldn't stop laughing.

Fred said, 'Excuse me, did you say your rollercoaster will be made today?'

'Yes, I guarantee you.'

I heard Grandma say to Fred, 'Let's hope Trendy Trev is not making it today.'

The greedy old man heard this remark and said, 'No, Trendy Trev has other things to be getting on with. My son Clever Trevor, with help from Trev the Third, who's my grandson, are making my rollercoaster today.'

Even Fred was laughing now.

Grandma said, 'Oh! Of course. I should've realised that's a job for Clever Trevor.'

'Oh, and before I forget to tell you, I'm a millionaire,' said the greedy old man.

Fred replied very quickly, 'So if we need a few lollypops, we know where to come.' Too

76

The greedy old man looked at Fred with an evil eye. 'Are you laughing at me?'

Fred, who could hardly speak for laughing, shook his head and said, 'What makes you think that?'

With that, the greedy old man walked away.

Grandma took a deep breath as if she was glad he had walked away so she could get her breath back, and Fred the same. Yazz, Kelvin and I couldn't speak for laughter. Even Kelvin, who is the most serious person you ever wish to meet, couldn't stop laughing.

Grandma looked over to Fred and quietly said, 'Let's just stay calm and hopefully we will be out of here as quick as possible. This greedy old man is full of self-importance, so we need to humour him and make him feel like he is wonderful, so we can get out of here.'

'You're right,' said Fred. 'Let's just get out of here'.

Just then, another guy walked up to the car, so Grandma then reminded us that we had to stay in the car no matter what.

The man looked like he needed a good wash. The greedy old man said, 'This is my son, Trusty Trev.'

We had only just stopped laughing about Clever Trevor. This was getting funnier and funnier.

Trusty Trev gestured at his father. 'He's a millionaire, you know, and one day I will inherit all this.'

Fred looked at the scruffy fellow and said, 'You must be the one they call Lucky.'

No, I'm not Lucky, I'm Trusty Trev.' He looked a bit puzzled by what Fred had said, as if he didn't understand what Fred meant, 'No, see, I'm not Lucky Trev. I'm Trusty Trev,' as if there was actually a Lucky Trev as well. I thought to myself, I wish there were a live audience. It all felt like a big joke, and then Trusty Trev carried on talking, telling us, 'To be able to inherit all this, I need to work very hard, every day and every night, and only then I can inherit Pleasure Island.'

Fred replied quickly again, 'I couldn't agree with you more there, Trusty Trev. Make sure you buy shares on a good skip company, because from where I'm standing it looks like you are going to inherit a load of rubbish.'

Trusty Trev was scratching his head, still looking very puzzled by Fred's replies. After a silence he replied to Fred, 'But you are sitting down.'

'Sorry, Trusty Trev. I meant to say from where I was sitting.'

It was as if Trusty Trev had been reading a script that the greedy old man had prepared for him. Once the script had all been said, Trusty Trev had nothing else to say and just stood looking at us, like a scarecrow.

The greedy old man was getting very annoyed with his son, Trusty Trev, and told him to go and pick up some rubbish somewhere.

Trusty Trev lifted his hands and started to shake them – it all looked very strange – and then said, 'I CAN DO ANYTHING, ME!' and off he went to pick up the rubbish.

The greedy old man was still holding his microphone, and Grandma was still slowly driving through the park. Fred said, 'Not long now, and we'll be out of here.'

Just then, another scruffy-looking guy walked up, and Daisy had to stop the car again because they would just walk in front of the car, so there was no choice but to stop.

'Hello,' he said. 'I'm a grandson. Name's Tricky Trev. I can see you've met my grandad. He's a millionaire, you know.'

Grandma said, 'I can't believe this. They all have the same script.'

Fred said, 'For Pete's sake, how many Trevs do you have?' Except this time it wasn't funny. It was getting boring now. Fred asked Tricky Trev if he could stand aside so we could move on.

Grandma started to drive slowly towards what looked like the way out. Then, out of nowhere, we all spotted a very smart young lad walking towards the car. This time, the young lad looked very important: he was wearing a lovely grey suit, a crisp white shirt, and a tie. We were all looking at him in amazement. Fred said, 'Finally! Somebody that looks sensible.'

The young man went straight towards Fred, and Grandma stopped the car at once.

Fred quickly put the car window down, the young man held out his hand, and Fred shook the young man's hand and said, 'Hello, I'm Fred. This my good friend Daisy.'

The young man replied, 'Hello, it's very nice to meet you. I'm Trev the Third, but you can call me Turd.'

Yazz, Kelvin and I thought this had to be the funniest part yet, and Yazz was almost crying with laughter. Fred went silent, slowly let go of the young man's hand and calmly rested his own hand on his knee. I noticed that when Fred had lowered his hand, he took a slight look at it, and I can only imagine he was checking for turd – even funnier!

Then the greedy old man reappeared. He said to Fred, 'I'm glad you've met Turd because he is my best worker and the only Trev with any brains.'

Fred said to Grandma, very quietly, 'And that's one they call Turd – and he's the brains of the bunch.'

The greedy old man went on, 'Yes, we call him Turd, because he is good at everything he does.'

Fred said to Grandma in a whisper, 'Please don't ask

79

what Trev the Third does, because we don't need to know.'
I could see Fred was very annoyed. It was as if they didn't
know the meaning of the word turd. To them, turd was a
great word, meaning something fantastic. *Well done, you
old turd.*

Just then, Trusty Trev had returned and he was carrying
two pieces of litter. The greedy old man said, 'What are
you doing with that litter in your hands? Looking for a bin?
We don't have bins here, just put it under that bench over
there.'

Trusty Trev replied, 'But it's already full of rubbish
under there.'

The old man was getting very angry. 'Just put in your
pocket, then!'

Trusty Trev shrugged and said, 'Okay.' Then he raised
his hands again, shook them, and said, 'I CAN DO
ANYTHING, ME!'

Yeah, I thought. Anything except find a place for the
rubbish.

Fred shouted out, 'Excuse me, sir!'

The greedy old man turned around and said, 'Okay, so
now you want to ride my new rollercoaster, yes?'

'No way!' said Grandma, looking over at the
rollercoaster, still in a big pile on the ground.

The greedy old man said, 'Turd is working on it now so
it shouldn't be much longer.'

We all looked around and yes, the very smart young lad
with a crisp white shirt had just started building up the
rollercoaster while wearing his lovely suit. Once again I
marvelled at the idea of Turd being the intelligent one.

The greedy old man, still using his microphone, asked
us if we would like to see his mansion.

Grandma, with a mischievous look in her eye,

whispered to Fred, 'I made it myself from natural resources.' The greedy old man wouldn't understand the meaning of 'natural resources'; the rest of us were thinking about turds.

'Yes,' said the greedy old man. 'I live in a mansion that I built myself using all the sand off the beach. Turd and I worked day and night to build my mansion.'

'This is getting worse,' Fred said to Grandma. Fred had realised just how to speak to the greedy old man, who was clearly a law unto himself. 'That sounds wonderful!' Fred said to the greedy old man. 'You are very lucky to live in a mansion. You must have more money than the King!'

The old man was very happy with Fred's comment. 'You're coming round to my way of thinking,' he said to Fred. He was so happy that he started dancing. 'I will show you my mansion. Follow me!'

Grandma was very pleased with Fred because we were now moving through the park and hopefully towards the exit. Because the old man was showing us his mansion, he had forgotten that all we really wanted to do was get out of the park. As we approached what the greedy old man was calling a mansion that he and Turd had made from natural resources, we noticed an old lady carrying what looked like a really heavy bag. Still using his microphone, the greedy old man called the old lady 'Blondielocks', and when we all looked at her closer, she had a mass of long blonde hair and she was really struggling with the heavy bag, but the old man made no attempt to help her. I felt really sorry for her – the bag was clearly too heavy for her to carry.

As she got nearer to the car, the greedy old man turned around and said to Blondielocks, 'Have you been steeling my money again?' Blondielocks went bright red, then he said to us, 'This is my Blondielocks. She looks after me and all my Trevs.' Blondielocks put down the heavy bag, looked at us all sat in the car, and smiled at us politely. The old man then turned to Blondielocks and said, 'Next time you are doing my ironing, please don't iron my underpants, because it makes them very uncomfortable for me to wear.'

Blondielocks looked at the old man and said, 'Okay.'

Then, still using his microphone whilst he was talking to her, the man asked, 'Where are you going with all those 2ps?'

'I'm going to pay your electricity bill.'

Still making no attempt to help her, the old man said, 'Don't be long.'

Blondielocks said, 'Okay, I will be as quick as possible.'

The old man said, 'Good, because when you get back, you still have the toilets to clean, don't forget.'

I was feeling really sorry for Blondielocks, as I realised that the greedy old man had no respect for anybody – not his sons, nor his grandsons, especially not dear old Blondielocks, who could not iron his underpants anymore. We had all had enough by now, nobody in the car was laughing anymore and we felt like the greedy old man was just terrible, and we couldn't wait to get away from him. As we got nearer to what he was calling his mansion, we all noticed the park's exit, but no one said anything because the old man might have heard us and closed the gate, so we needed to play it safe.

Fred said to Grandma, 'Right, on my signal, you head for that exit. Put your foot down, and don't stop until we're out of here.' By then, we were sat in front of the mansion – if you could call it that; it looked more like a derelict hotel that had been patched up, and you could clearly see he had been using the sand off the beach to do the patching because the bricks were all falling out, and Fred said that was because of the salt in the sand, and this would eventually rot all the bricks and it would all fall down.

Yazz said, 'I hope Blondielocks isn't in there when that happens.'

The old man was standing in front of the mansion telling us over the loudspeaker how he was lord of his mansion. Fred was losing his patience again and said to us, 'Mansion? It looks more like a haunted house. Remember what I told you, Daisy. On my signal.'

'I'm ready,' Grandma replied.

'Not long now,' said Fred, 'and we will be out of here.'

The old man then walked over to our car, still holding the microphone, which I'm sure was glued to his hand. Grandma's window was already down, and the old man started to explain how hard he had been working all his life and never stopped, not even on Christmas Day.

Grandma replied, 'We all have to play our part in this life.'

The greedy old man seemed to really like Grandma's reply. 'Yes,' he agreed. 'Yes, you are right. We must all work hard, very hard.'

Then something WEIRD happened: Grandma's hand was tightly holding the steering wheel of the car waiting for Fred's signal, and then the greedy old man put his hand on top of Grandma's hand and said, 'BUT SOMETIMES YOU CAN BE LUCKY AND SOMEBODY MIGHT LEAVE YOU SOMETHING WHEN THEY DIE!'

Grandma was shocked by what the greedy old man had said to her and quickly pulled her hand away and replied sternly, 'I would prefer everybody to survive and I WILL MAKE MY OWN WAY THANK YOU.'

The greedy man was not expecting that, and in reply he just raised his arms in the air, waving them about as if to dismiss us, and then said, 'I'm going to count all my money now.'

He turned his back on us, and Fred said, 'Go! Go!' and Grandma did just that. I never realised Grandma was such a good driver – the car was like a rocket.

Grandma headed straight for the gate and we never stopped, nor did we look back. We were finally leaving Pleasure Island – it seemed like we had been there forever. Grandma and Fred had a look of relief on their faces. And just like that, we were finally off the island. We could all breathe a sigh of relief. As we went through the gates of the park, all we could see in front of us was miles and miles of beautiful beach, with miles and miles of sand – it was like paradise. Once we could no longer see the island, Grandma stopped the car, we all went silent for a few seconds. I cannot explain the feeling of relief we all felt. Even Kelvin was laughing with relief.

Yazz said, 'Did that really just happen?'

Grandma replied, 'Yes, and thankfully only on this journey will you ever meet such a greedy old man, because surely no such person exists elsewhere.'

Fred said, 'Never in my life have I ever met such a silly old fool. I hope I never have to meet him again.'

Yazz said, 'I felt sorry for Blondielocks. She looked exhausted.'

'Yes, I agree,' said Grandma. 'She looked completely worn out, as if she had been worked to a frazzle, as if she had been digging for gold.'

Fred said, laughing, 'Well, I think she will be digging for a long time.'

'Okay, children, we're on the last leg of this journey. Kelvin, what's the time?'

It's what the clock reads on the dashboard, Grandma. We have reached Horsey Gap, and it's 16.42, and we are back in the UK, so that means it's 17.42 in Sweden and 18.42 in Finland.' I could tell Kelvin was really pleased to have put the island behind him. We shared the same opinion – that there wasn't anything pleasurable about Pleasure Island.

Fred said, 'Let's make a move, Daisy.'

'Yes, of course, let's get moving.'

We were on the beach and in front of us was the most beautiful view: sea and sand, and that's all you could see – it was like a breath of fresh air. We all felt free, free from the grip of the greedy old man. Grandma started the road trip again, but this time there wasn't any advice from Ralph, or the soldier in his immaculate uniform. This time, Grandma was driving in the dark, as she put it – not literally but without guidance.

'Now, remember, children – keep your eyes open,' she said. Grandma was only driving slowly. After a few minutes we could hear something coming up behind us. Grandma looked in her rear view mirror and we all turned to look and see what it was. This journey was never going to cease to amaze us. You couldn't even imagine the magnificence that we were all looking at in this moment in time. The cavalry was coming up behind us,

Fred said, 'Stop the car, Daisy, and let them pass us, and then we can follow them.'

'But we don't know where they are going,' Grandma replied.

Fred said, 'I know, but I just feel it's the right thing to do. We don't know which way to go.'

Grandma replied in a quick tone of voice, 'There is only one way to go.'

Fred looked around and said, 'Yes, you're right, so let's just stay behind. I'll feel more comfortable behind than in front.'

'Yes, me too,' said Daisy. 'I will just go slow and stay back so as not to spook the horses, and let them pass us by.'

We had never seen the cavalry before. Dad had told us many times how magnificent they looked riding their horses, but nothing could prepare us for such splendour.

Once again everyone in the car was silent as they came past us. The soldiers' uniforms were perfect: the gold braiding with the gold buttons against the navy blue was outstanding. The black riding boots were so shiny you could see reflections in them. They were also carrying swords. The horses were very tall and so well-groomed. The first soldier to pass by us was wearing the hackle, a white feather upon his hat. As he went past the car, he looked down towards us and raised his hand and nodded his head as to suggest a thank-you. I can only imagine that this was because Grandma had stopped the car to let them pass.

The soldiers were riding in twos side by side and I counted twenty pairs in total. Kelvin was fascinated and never said much, and Yazz looked very impressed.

Grandma said, 'What grandeur!'

Fred said 'This journey has not failed to surprise us at every turn. I would say that anything is possible in the land of the good Witch Matilda.'

Yazz said, 'Matilda the witch! I had forgotten all about her! This journey has been fantastic up to now.'

I replied, 'I don't want this journey to end.'

Kelvin said, 'I miss Mum and Dad. I want to go home.'

Grandma said, 'It's not much further now, Kelvin, and I'm sure we will be there really soon.'

Grandma was still following the cavalry, and we were still on the beach and still looking at the most beautiful view of the sea and sand with blue sky.

Fred said, 'If paradise is a real place, I think we have found it, Daisy.' Grandma nodded.

Yazz said, 'What's that up ahead?'

We all looked. Up on the horizon, there was the outline of a building, As we continued following the cavalry, the nearer we got, and the bigger the building became.

Grandma said, 'What on earth is that building? It looks like a large collection of shoeboxes.'

I looked too, and yes it was very square but also very slightly breathtaking! If I'm honest, I found it hard to take my eyes off the building. The vastness was staggering, and I couldn't wait to get closer.

Yazz asked, 'Is that where the witch lives?'

Fred replied, 'It could be her alcazar.'

As we got nearer, the cavalry sped up and moved away from us, leaving us a clear view. We were now within full view of the alcazar and it was magnificent, clearly for a special person.

Fred said, 'I have never seen anything so big! Its enormity is beyond belief.'

Grandma wasn't so impressed. 'Too square for me.'

Yazz said, 'Grandma, yes it is very square, but it's most definitely got the wow factor.'

'Oh yes, Yazz it's definitely got the wow factor,' replied Grandma.

Kelvin asked, 'Will we have to go inside? Because I didn't want to go inside.'

I could sense that Kelvin was feeling very uncomfortable. I told him, 'Don't worry. I will stay with you all the time. We will wait in the car.' With that in mind, Kelvin looked happier.

I couldn't take my eyes off the alcazar. It was all glass, which glistened in the sunlight, shining like a new pin, gleaming the most beautiful colour of green I have ever seen. The more you looked, the more you wanted to see, like a magnet drawing me in. I noticed that I couldn't see a door, nor any windows. Grandma was right about it being square – that's how the alcazar looked, but the boxy shapes were standing on their edge and slightly tilted outwards. However, I thought it looked great, and all I wanted to do was to get inside.

The nearer we got the more anxious Kelvin became, and I could see Grandma and Fred were starting to worry about him. Fred told Grandma to stop the car, then once the car was at a standstill Fred suggested that we all get out and take a minute. Fred was right – we needed to stop and take a moment to think about what will happen next. This was also just what Kelvin needed. The sound of the waves hitting the beach was calming, and it was what we all needed – a moment to catch our breath and think 'What next?'. Even though the sea was deep blue in colour and crystal clear and the beautiful waves were crashing down on the golden sand, the only thing we could look at was this massive alcazar, which was so big it seemed to be consuming everything in sight – nothing could compare to it. It was all we could look at; nothing else seemed to matter – not the beautiful sea, nor the golden sand and clear blue sky. This alcazar was overshadowing it all with its enormity.

The grandest part was – and I never thought I would say

such a thing – the clockface in the centre of the alcazar, which was also the tallest part of the structure. The clock, like the alcazar, was also massive. Its large face was purple, with silver makers and silver hands.

Kelvin was delighted with the clock and he asked Fred, 'Fred, would you know the size of that clockface?'

Fred took a deep breath and said, 'From where we are standing, it's hard to say, but at an estimate, I would say 30 metres in diameter.'

We all just stood looking at it in amazement, transfixed.

Grandma said to Fred, 'What do you think is in that alcazar? Mr Fudge never mentioned this part of the journey, did he?'

We were all now hoping that this was Witch Matilda's home. But I felt unsettled – what if it wasn't? What if there was much more journey ahead of us?

Fred replied, 'I suppose Mr Fudge thought the journey would be the hardest part, and the most important.'

'Yes, I agree with that,' said Grandma, 'and I suppose nothing could prepare us for this anyway.'

By that time, the cavalry had lined up in front of the alcazar if they were standing guard. But I still couldn't see a door. 'Yazz,' I said, 'can you see the door?'

She replied, 'Something as big as this wouldn't have a door, it would have to be an entrance or a gate.' But neither I nor Yazz could see an entrance.

Grandma said, 'I would imagine the entrance is under the clock.'

Kelvin had calmed down and now focused all his attention on the clock face.

Grandma explained how the next part of our journey was to try and gain entry so we could see the witch. 'Not having any guidance,' she continued, 'we don't know what to expect, and we don't know what's coming next, so Kelvin, please try and stay calm as much as you can,

Kelvin replied, 'Grandma, I will just focus all my energy on the clock, because that's the biggest clock I've ever seen, but if I start to get anxious, I'm sorry.'

Grandma replied, 'Good idea, Kelvin. Just focus your energy on the clock, and don't worry.' Then she turned to me. 'Max, as always, keep your eyes wide open. And you too, Yazz.'

'Grandma, how are we going to get in?' I asked.

Grandma said, 'That we don't know, but once we get nearer to the alcazar, we should be able to work it out.'

'Okay,' said Kelvin, slightly nervous.

We all got back into the car and Grandma started driving slowly towards the alcazar once again, heading towards the centre of the building. As we got nearer the building, the cavalry started to separate, half one side and half the other, as if they were guiding us towards the centre of the alcazar. As we drove on, we were all getting anxious, nervous, excited, and all these emotions felt like they were spinning around the car so intensely you could almost touch them.

'Look, Grandma!'

'What, Max? What?' she said nervously

'I can see the entrance!'

The entrance was starting to open, and it was as we predicted: in the centre of the alcazar, directly under the giant clock. It was now clear to see we were able the drive the car inside. Grandma aimed directly below the clock and just kept driving slowly. We were all still anxious and excited. At the same time, it felt like the inside of the car was melting, almost like the nearer we got, the more invisible the car became. The alcazar was starting to consume us and the car. We finally drove through the entrance, and it was as if we all took a deep breath together and nobody dared say one word. And just like that, we were inside.

Grandma stopped the car. 'That wasn't so difficult,' she said, in a surprised tone. We sat in amazement for a few moments, looking around. The inside was just as impressive as the outside, only now *we* were being consumed by its enormity.

After what seemed a lifetime, Fred said, 'Do you think we should get out of the car?'

Grandma replied, 'No, not until we see someone.'

Yazz said, 'And keep your fingers crossed it's not the greedy old man!'

I felt myself wanting to laugh but I was too nervous.

Kelvin hadn't said one word or counted one number. He was just looking around in amazement like the rest of us. Kelvin told me that this was because he had noticed that high up in the roof, fixed so they were facing downwards, there were lots and lots of clocks, and that's why Kelvin was silent – he was staring at all the clocks. They were from all around the world, showing the different times from everywhere. Each clock had the name of each town, city and country. The alcazar's interior was very grand: marble, gold, crystal, large oak-panelled doors, large chandeliers sparkling like crystal in the bright sun. Altogether, it looked like a palace from the grand Victorian era, quite a contrast to the outside, which looked more Art Deco – shoeboxes, as Grandma put it. Grandma and Fred were clearly very impressed by what they were looking at. In front of them was a massive staircase, which started as one at the bottom and then separated left and right, then climbed to the roof. At the top of the staircase, you were able to gain access to all the clocks using a network of walkways.

Just then I noticed someone walking towards the car, and then I recognised them. 'Grandma!' I called out. 'It's Ralph!'

We all felt so happy to see a familiar face. Even though we had only met Ralph today, I was glad he was here, and it made us feel a lot less anxious. Even Grandma was pleased to see Ralph. Ralph was walking towards us with a big smile on his face and could no doubt see we were all pleased to see him, and he looked pleased to see us.

Now that we could see Ralph, we decided to get out of the car.

Ralph said to us, 'I'm glad you made it.'

Grandma said, 'Yes, it's quite a journey.'

'Yes,' he said. 'The journey of a lifetime. That's what Witch Matilda calls it.'

Fred said, 'So, Ralph, is this Witch Matilda's alcazar?'

'Yes,' said Ralph. 'The Good Witch Matilda's alcazar, and you have now reached the destination of the alcazar at Horsey Gap. I applaud you!' Ralph started to clap his hands. 'Would you like me to show you around?'

Grandma, being Grandma, said, 'Have we got time?'

Ralph looked at Grandma with that big smile and said, 'We will make time.'

Grandma knew exactly what Ralph was thinking, and she just smiled back.

Fred asked Ralph, 'Will the car be okay there?'

Ralph laughed. 'We don't have traffic wardens here. Yes, that's fine.'

I asked Ralph, 'Why is this called an alcazar?'

'The word alcazar is Spanish for palace,' Ralph explained.

'So, is Witch Matilda Spanish?'

'Her mother was Spanish.'

I nodded. 'Is Witch Matilda at home?'

'Yes, Matilda is home, but she's not ready to see you yet.'

Kelvin was still looking at all the clocks and timing them to make sure they were in time; he was in his element. Grandma and Fred looked relieved to see Kelvin so content.

Fred asked Ralph, 'Is there anything we need to know at this stage? Before we meet Witch Matilda?'

Ralph replied, 'When Matilda stands before you, just let her speak, and after Matilda has finished, she will ask you questions. Witch Matilda already knows why you are here, so there's no need to explain. Just wait for her to ask the questions. Never talk at Witch Matilda, Matilda knows why you are here. Witch Matilda likes conversation – the exchange of thoughts and words on the matters that stand before you – in your case, Winston. Witch Matilda will want to explore your mind to ensure that you are aware of your actions.'

Yazz asked Ralph, 'What do you mean when you say talk at her?'

'Well, it's like this. A conversation is a two-way thing. As well as speaking, you must listen. No one person can know everything. Witch Matilda doesn't like people who are full of self-importance and have no interest in others.'

I quickly replied, 'Like the greedy old man?'

Ralph said, 'Exactly, Max. The greedy old man.' He laughed. 'Did you get along okay with the greedy old man?'

'NO,' we all said at the same time.

Ralph laughed again. 'Not to worry. Nobody can get

along with him. He is everything that Witch Matilda dislikes.'

I asked, 'How will Witch Matilda know we are not like the greedy old man?'

'Because you did all you could to get away from him and get off the island – and that was your test. Witch Matilda believes that birds of a feather flock together.'

Yazz whispered to Fred, 'What does that mean?'

Fred replied, 'A group of people with the same ideas, and that can be anything from playing bowls to football, or getting up to good or bad things. Birds of a feather all have the same things in common.'

Ralph then showed us around the immediate area, which was stunning. I felt so lucky to be in Witch Matilda's alcazar. Grandma and Fred never said very much about alcazar, but you could clearly see the amazement on their faces. Grandma was much more impressed with the inside than the outside.

After we had taken in our surroundings, Ralph kind of moved away from us, though not out of sight. It was as if he had taken up his position in readiness for something, and he had a look of anticipation on his face. He never said anything of the sort, but we just got that feeling. Then the alcazar seemed to go slightly darker. We never said anything to each other, but we just knew, and without realising it, we had moved closer together. The alcazar was vast that even the car looked so small inside it. I thought to myself, I like this alcazar – this place really suits the word alcazar, because calling it a palace would seem too old-fashioned, and it was definitely too big to be called a house, and it wasn't a castle because there weren't any towers. So, alcazar – that was perfect, and it sounded much more impressive than any other name. I could see

Grandma and Fred were getting slightly anxious. Fred's eyes kept flicking nervously to Ralph.

Grandma shouted out to Ralph, 'Why are you standing over there?'

Ralph replied, 'This is where Witch Matilda likes me to stand.'

Fred started to look a bit more anxious, and he shouted to Ralph, 'Where should we stand, Ralph?'

'Just where you are. Don't worry – you have good reason to be here, and Witch Matilda understands why you have made this journey.'

Grandma, who had literally been the driving force in getting us to Horsey Gap, was now standing aside, and Fred seemed more in control than Grandma at this point. Grandma was standing by the driver's side of the car with Kelvin by her side, as if she was getting ready to leave. I thought to myself, yesterday Grandma couldn't tell us enough about Witch Matilda, and we were all deeply enthralled; now, truth be told, we were all slightly afraid of what was going to happen. I started to shake slightly as if I was cold – but I wasn't cold because the alcazar felt warm. I looked over at Grandma. She had gone very pale-faced. Kelvin, however, for the first time on this journey, was just fine, as if he was very comfortable with his surroundings. It almost looked like Kelvin had been here before. Kelvin had a look of confidence about him that I had never noticed before. The alcazar seemed as if it was Kelvin's kind of place.

Yazz had gone completely silent, as if shock was taking over her. I didn't say anything to her, nor she to me. Fred was restless – not saying anything, but couldn't stand still, like a child in a sweet shop who just wanted his sweets so that he could leave the shop to eat the sweets.

It was going to happen any minute, I thought. Then, second thoughts, *what* was going to happen? Now we were at the alcazar I felt as if we had done something wrong, and I also had the sense that Grandma, Fred and Yazz felt the same, but not Kelvin. Kelvin seemed very happy, and for the life of me I couldn't work out why.

Still thinking to myself whether we should really be there, I then remembered why we were there: because Grandma wanted to try and help the gardener. For a moment I had forgotten this. I suppose the journey had temporarily consumed my thoughts.

And then we heard a stern, deep tone of voice, very commanding. 'Welcome to my alcazar.'

Everybody knew Witch Matilda was here, but we couldn't see her.

'I congratulate you, Ralph, for bringing my visitors here safely. Tell me, were my visitors easy to deal with?'

I looked straight at Grandma. Grandma looked straight at Ralph, and I could see Grandma knew if Ralph was going to complain at all, it would be about her.

Thankfully, Ralph looked at Grandma, smiled and said, 'No, everybody was quite pleasant.'

Witch Matilda was speaking to Ralph as if we weren't there, which made me feel invisible and somehow more comfortable. Grandma and Fred didn't seem so comfortable. I looked over at Grandma and she was looking increasingly anxious, so I smiled nicely. Yazz was shaking.

Witch Matilda, still talking to Ralph, said, 'Were there any problems I should know about?'

'No problems. The journey went smoothly.'

'Very good,' said Witch Matilda. 'So I have a very obedient group here? Would you say that, Ralph?'

'Yes, most definitely. All instructions were followed carefully.' I thought how kind Ralph was to summarise it like that.

Witch Matilda replied, 'That's all I need to know. You can leave now, Ralph.' We all looked at each other. We didn't want Ralph to leave. It felt like we were all walking into the woods at night without a torch, and you just could see what was coming next. Before Ralph left, he said, with his big smile on his face, 'I must leave you all now.'

We all reluctantly said goodbye to Ralph.

He replied 'Not goodbye – see you later.'

Witch Matilda, who seemed to be standing on what looked like a bandstand, the type you see in a public park sometimes, turned her attention to Fred. At the same time, the black crow with the green eyes landed beside her. I thought to myself, I knew the crow was following us.

'Hello, Fred,' Matilda said. 'It's been a long time since you and your friend Jim almost ended up in my walled garden. May I ask why you thought it okay to visit my garden without my permission?'

Fred was speechless. He hadn't thought that the witch would speak to him, let alone mention the night he and Grandad Jim almost visited the walled garden. Fred had a look of shock horror on his face. He muttered, 'Oh ... um ... well, you see, I was only young then.'

The witch replied, 'Young, yes you were. Nevertheless, you were aware that what you were doing was wrong?' Fred was still looking for some words to come out of his mouth. The witch went on, 'And yet you still tried to get in.'

Then Fred seemed to straighten up, and he replied with a defiant tone of voice, 'Yes, we did. And it was all my idea. You see, Jim accidentally kicked his ball over into the walled garden. Jim was very worried that his parents were going to find out, because Jim's parents had always warned him to stay away from the walled garden, but I was very curious and insisted we get the ball back somehow. Jim was very reluctant.'

Witch Matilda replied, 'Well, Fred, you know what they say about curiosity.'

Fred replied, 'Yes, I understand, and I would like to apologise to you. I'm sorry.'

To our relief, Witch Matilda said, 'I accept your apology.'

As she stepped down from the bandstand, we got our first clear view of her as she came into full view. Witch Matilda was tall, with long auburn hair. Her skin was olive, and her eyes were emerald-green, and breath-taking. They were two brilliant gems piercing through your brain when she looked your way. Witch Matilda had the most beautiful emerald-green dress, which Grandma told me afterwards she thought was made from duchess satin and was three quarter length, with sleeves that sat just above the elbows. The dress had a stand collar and the waistband was encrusted with emerald crystals. The dress was as beautiful as Witch Matilda herself. Her hat was black, tall and pointed with the most beautiful peacock feathers. The witch was beautiful. She wasn't how I imagined her to look. Witch Matilda was more beautiful and stylish than I could have ever imagined. Yazz, Kelvin, Grandma and Fred looked just as impressed as I was. I remembered once hearing my mum use the expression jaw-dropping, and now I knew what she meant.

Then the witch turned her attention to Grandma. 'So, Daisy, you have your theory?'

Grandma replied very nervously, 'Yes.'

The witch went on, 'Winston has been a great asset to your village for more years than I care to think about. Winston has made the walled garden his life, his complete life, and asked for nothing in return, only that he can spend every minute possible in my garden. And yes, it is with an heavy heart and much regret that it falls upon me to have to inform you that the two children that got lost through the secret gate are Winston's children – two little girls. Now, you tell me: what do you think you can do about that?'

Grandma said, 'I came all this way because Winston has been so loyal to the village, and we owe it to him to try and help. What kind of people would we be if we didn't do that. How can I and my grandchildren live the rest of our lives with peace of mind knowing the lost children belong to Winston?'

Witch Matilda said, 'You have a good point, and I know exactly how you would feel, because believe me when I say I have tried my hardest to get those children back for many years. Look at all the clocks I have installed. I have been tracking the time all over the world and trying to find the safest way to bring back the children without losing anybody else. But without the timekeeper, it's impossible.' I sensed anger in her voice. 'So tell me,' she continued, 'have you brought me the timekeeper?'

I looked at Kelvin. He had a glow about him, the look on his face, and his ears were probably already ringing, like they did every time he got excited.

Grandma looked straight at Kelvin. Kelvin nodded his head as if to say yes, then Grandma turned to the witch and said very confidently, 'Yes, we have brought you a timekeeper.'

Witch Matilda turned very quickly and looked straight

at Grandma. She hadn't been expecting that answer. 'Tell me, who is the timekeeper?'

Kelvin stepped forward, raised his hand and said, 'I'm the timekeeper.' I felt so proud of Kelvin. I felt like shouting out loud, 'He's my brother!' Kelvin was standing so tall and important.

Witch Matilda walked straight over to Kelvin and said, 'Kelvin – that's your name?'

'Yes.'

'Tell me, Kelvin, what is the time at this precise moment in St Louis, USA?'

Kelvin replied very quickly, '10.57.'

'And Alexandria, Egypt?'

'18.57.'

'Sydney, Australia?'

'03.57.'

'Araguaia, Brazil?'

'13.58.'

'Aktobe, Kazakhstan?'

'21.58.'

As Witch Matilda went back and forth across the world, and Kelvin never failed. As quick as Matilda asked Kelvin the times, he was just as quick with every reply and so confident. Yazz and I were so impressed, and we felt very proud of our brother. Witch Matilda tried very hard to catch Kelvin out, but he was not faltering, nor was he hesitating to answer. Grandma and even Fred had a look of disbelief on their faces – not because Grandma would ever doubt Kelvin, but because Witch Matilda was so intense, like a flamethrower. But Kelvin never let the heat bother him, not even for a split second. He fired back the answers just as intensely. Finally, Witch Matilda got through her list of chosen time zones, and then she asked the question,

'Do you think you can safely travel through time without getting lost in time, tracking every second, Kelvin?'

Kelvin replied, 'If you can get me to the correct time zone, I'm sure I would be able to get back to the gate in time.'

Witch Matilda went silent. We could all see she went into deep thought. We stood again in silence, all looking at each other. Then, after what seemed a very long pause, she said, 'Our first problem will be that much time has passed since the children went through the secret gate, and that could be a problem. They may be grown up, or they may be still the same age if we get the timing right.'

'Our second problem,' she continued, 'will be that Winston is very old, so the children may not even recognise their own father, and that would have a devastating impact on Winston. I will have to think about how we could achieve our goal.' Witch Matilda sat down, and I could see that look of deep thought was weighing down again on her. Then I had an idea, so I put my hand up as if I was at school, and Witch Matilda looked at me and asked, 'Why have you raised your hand, young man?'

I quickly replied, 'May I speak to you?'

'You may, but firstly, what is your name?'

I took a deep breath and replied, 'Max.'

Matilda looked at me very curiously and said, 'Yes, please do tell me what is on your mind.'

'Can you make a spell to bring back the children? As you are a great witch, and I know you have done this before.'

Matilda looked at me and smiled, and then said, 'If I could create a spell to bring back those children, I would have done that many years ago, but it's impossible. Max, I will let you in on a secret – spells are best suited to the bad people of the world, because they partly help to create the spells themselves by being unkind to others in one way or the other. For instance, when I cast the spell on your village many, many years ago, all that was needed for that spell to work was to remove the gardener from the walled garden and let the garden all overgrow, making sure the nettles took hold. That was not a spell – it was the mess the villagers had created themselves, so I just needed to make my presence known and lead the villagers to believe they had upset me, which worked perfectly. Many of them knew that what they had done was very wrong – you could call it the spell of conscience – and I was just highlighting it. And that, my young Max, is how my spell worked, and worked it did. Being unkind to others for your own selfish need is not the correct way to achieve your goals in life. You all met the greedy old man. Tell me, young Max, what did your young mind think of such a person?'

I stood in silence and amazement. I couldn't believe I was standing here, and Witch Matilda was asking me, yes me, the question. No words were coming to mind, but in my mind the words 'strange, ungenuine, very bossy' floated around. And then something just popped into my head: 'The greedy old man is a spiteful man.'

'Well done, young Max,' said Witch Matilda. 'That is a very good way to describe the greedy old man. Spiteful. So, if I was going to cast a spell onto the greedy old man, the spell would need to be a spiteful spell in order to work.'

'Please may I ask,' I ventured, 'if the island used to be nice, and if everybody was happy living and working there? We were told it was a very prosperous place, and now it looks so sad and dirty. How did the greedy old man manage to become part of what was once a beautiful place?'

Witch Matilda looked at me and smiled. 'You are very intelligent, young Max. I will tell you. Please listen carefully. First, the greedy old man used all of his cunning stills to create a diversion. Once the diversion was in place, he managed to buy the last green space left on the island, and turn the space into a park before anybody really noticed. Once the other traders found out what he had done, they were furious with the previous owner of the green space for selling it to the man. But the man had promised the previous owner that the green space would remain the same, and that he would spend millions of pounds looking after and maintaining the park, with the promise of millions of pounds of investment, which in fact wasn't needed. But the greedy old man needed to win over all the other traders and residents, so he made up stories of past times, creating an illusion, and promising grander times to come now that he was in charge of the park. What came next was lie after lie – in fact, years and years of lies. The greedy old man is a disgrace. And all these years later, now everybody has realised the mistake they have all made, they can see he had conned them all into believing he was the greatest showman on the earth, and now it's too late. The greedy old man will not leave the island, and there is nothing anyone can do, because he is the owner. The traders' biggest mistake was not realising how good things were. They took their lives and businesses for granted.'

I asked, 'What was the illusion?'

'Empty promises. The greedy old man studied what they already had and what they were most happy with, and simply promised the same but much better. Later, after they all realised what they had done, the island was never the same, visitors stopped visiting, and one by one all the

103

traders left and all the residents moved off the island, leaving the greedy old man to own everything, just how he planned it. The lesson is: never, ever judge a book by its cover. If they had researched the greedy old man, they would've found out he was a liar and a thief with a criminal record.'

I told Witch Matilda, 'I hope that I never see the greedy old man again.'

Witch Matilda replied, 'Wise words, young Max.' She then turned her attention to Yazz. 'Hello. Please tell me your name.'

'Yazz is my name.'

'Tell me, Yazz, what do you think about bringing the children and Winston back together?'

Yazz replied, 'All my thoughts are with the children. I'm very lucky. I have my mum and dad, plus a fantastic grandma – all the support I could ever wish for. I would have loved to have spent time with my grandad, Jim, and my mum's parents, but they all passed away when I was young, so I don't have any memories of them. I spend lots of time thinking about them, and I love to hear the stories about their lives. My point is, if I could spend one hour of past times with my grandparents, I would enjoy every minute.'

Witch Matilda nodded sympathetically.

Yazz asked, 'How old were the children when they went through the gate?'

Witch Matilda replied, 'They were seven and nine.'

Yazz said, 'So, they would have been old enough to remember their parents.'

'Yes,' said Matilda, 'and that's what makes this so hard.' After a pause, she added, 'Yazz, what do you think we should do?'

Yazz thought for a moment and replied, 'It's now obvious that the children are lost, and their sadness must be overwhelming, but the truth is we don't really know, and before we involve Winston, is it possible to check out the situation first? That way, there will not be any unnecessary upset for Winston to endure.'

'That is a very good and considerate thought, Yazz,' said Witch Matilda. 'Daisy, you started this journey, and in one sense I'm very grateful because I have only had myself to share this burden with, so please, tell me, what do you think we should do?'

Grandma stood in silence for a brief moment and then said, 'When I started this journey, I didn't release that there could be any difficulties. I just thought we would open the secret gate and bring the children back. I suppose I've been selfish, because even though my initial thought was only for Winston, I know now that I haven't put enough thought into the impact all this will have on Winston, nor was I thinking of the difficulties that we might come across. I just felt like I needed to do something to help. So I'm with Yazz on this – we should try to check the status of the girls before we involve Winston any further.' Grandma put her head down and clutched her hands together as if she were praying.

Witch Matilda said, 'It's called consequences, and consequences come in all shapes and forms, and the only cure for consequences is time. Time is the most precious thing in the world. Time cannot be bought nor sold and shouldn't be wasted. Every day we wake up is a signal that we have more precious time to spend, and you must always spend your time wisely. Today you have travelled the long journey that I laid out for you. You have seen many things and met a few people along the way. The journey was actually only twenty-five miles, but because there was so much to see, it seemed to take a long time. In fact, it only took an hour and twenty minutes to reach Horsey Gap from when you left the school, but because there was so much to see, the time seemed to last longer. The point I'm trying to make is that for you, today has been a good day because not a minute has been wasted up to now. Now, the consequences of your journey and the decisions you have taken to help Winston find his children are in fact a lot more complicated than you could ever have imagined. Although your intentions are very good, the consequences could be too big to deal with, so Daisy, the question is, can you handle the consequences of your actions?'

Grandma replied, 'What choice do I have?'

'There is always a choice, Daisy. You were brave to make the decision to visit me.'

Grandma replied, 'Then I will have to be brave enough to make the next step. The answer to your question is yes, I'm ready to face the consequences, no matter how hard they may be. I can see now that I have followed my instinct. It is my instinct that has brought me here. Right or wrong, I couldn't turn back how I will deal with the consequences.'

Witch Matilda said, 'Daisy, just remember, your time is precious.' Then she addressed all of us again. 'Let's not waste another minute. We must make our way back to the village.'

Fred asked, 'Will we have to take the same journey back?'

'No,' said Witch Matilda. 'We will follow the purple path straight back to the village. It's much quicker. I recommend you drive, Fred, as you have experience of the power of the purple path.'

Grandma said, 'I don't think we will all fit in my car, especially with that beautiful dress you're wearing.'

Witch Matilda replied, 'You will follow me. I will use my broomstick.'

I couldn't help myself and shouted out loud, 'You've got a broomstick?'

Witch Matilda turned and looked at me and smiled. Her smile lit up the alcazar like a beacon of light. I felt like I was a lost ship at sea, not knowing which way to sail, and then out of nowhere the glow of a lighthouse appeared on the horizon, with a sense of relief rushing over me, that feeling that you get when you realise everything is going to be okay.

Witch Matilda's smile was that powerful and that perfect, and I felt as if just one glance from her emerald-green eyes she could end a war.

'Yes, I have a broomstick. In fact, I have many, including some with two seats. Would you like to join me, young Max?'

'Yes please!' I felt so excited at just the thought of riding on a broomstick.

Grandma looked over at me and said, 'If you're riding on the broomstick, make sure you hold tight.'

Witch Matilda turned to Fred and said, 'Once you're all in the car, I will lead the way to the purple path. Remember, Fred, you will travel much faster on the purple path. It's like a vacuum. Your journey home will be very quick, so stay close.'

Fred replied with an excited tone of voice, 'I will.' Fred also had a look of relief on his face, as if the witch had made friends with Fred and now he was back in the game.

'Follow me, young Max. We are going to the broom cupboard.'

We walked over to a very tall set of double doors with big brass handles. Witch Matilda pulled open the doors and inside was the best collection of broomsticks you could ever imagine, all sitting on their own rack, just like bike racks. Some of them had one seat, some had two seats. Every broom was purple and emerald-green with black bristles and peacock feathers – just like the feathers on her hat. The broom handles were long and thin, and the paintwork was very shiny, with impressive artwork. Matilda patted one and I saw that it had two seats.

With everybody back in the car, Witch Matilda asked me, 'Are you ready, young Max?'

'Ready when you are.'

'We must sit on the broomstick whilst it's sat on the rack.'

I climbed onto the seat using the handle to keep my balance. Witch Matilda turned her seat slightly sideways and elegantly sat down. once we were both on board, the black crow with the green eyes swooped down and gently placed himself upon the broomstick and with that, the broom started to move very slowly. Witch Matilda turned around to face the car and shouted, 'Follow me, Fred!'

The alcazar was so big that Fred was able to easily drive Grandma's car around to follow Matilda. As we approached the purple path, I thought how it looked too nice to stand on, never mind drive a car along. It was so shiny, and as the car drove on the path it seemed to light up. The path seemed to be taking us underground. It was as if it was a secret passage out of the alcazar, and apart from the light coming from the purple path, there weren't any other lights. Then, as we approached the tunnel, Witch Matilda turned on a bright light on the front of the broomstick that guided us through the tunnel. Just like

Witch Matilda told Fred, the path was very fast. And then, there was a light at the end of the tunnel – day light. And just like that, we were out of the tunnel, travelling over land.

Witch Matilda seemed to be enjoying her ride on the broomstick. 'Faster! Faster!' she was shouting. The broomstick was going up and down. I felt like I was riding a rollercoaster, at the same time holding on for my life. I had been on a rollercoaster before so I knew the feeling, but this was much better because there weren't any tracks, so you couldn't see the next twists, turns, ups and downs. Witch Matilda was in control, and she loved it more than me. As we got out of the tunnel, I looked back and I couldn't see the alcazar any more. It was out of sight. The purple path was a different route – not the way we had gone to Horsey Gap.

I looked down and I could see Grandma's car. Fred was driving very fast, trying to keep up with Witch Matilda. The car looked so small from up there. Yazz and Kelvin were waving at me, but I was holding on so tight, I couldn't wave back. And then up ahead I could see our village. I felt happy. It seemed like I'd been away for a long time. I felt like I needed to see Mum and Dad. It was the first time I had missed them since they left three days ago.

Witch Matilda was heading straight for the walled garden. As we got nearer, it lit up as if the garden was coming to life at the arrival of Witch Matilda. I was enjoying the ride and didn't want it to end. Riding on the broomstick was amazing.

We landed smoothly at the entrance to the walled garden. Witch Matilda was glad to see that Winston was not at home, as this way we would be able to see into the secret gate before we mentioned our intentions to

Winston. I looked at Witch Matilda and asked if it was okay for us to go inside. Witch Matilda replied, 'You are with me, young Max, so the answer to your question is yes. But we must wait for Daisy, Fred, Kelvin and Yazz.'

Witch Matilda unlocked the gate to the walled garden. As I turned to look back I could see Grandma, Fred, Kelvin and Yazz, who had just arrived. Fred parked the car outside Winston's house, and they all got out of the car and stood looking down at me and Witch Matilda. I could see Fred was reluctant to walk down to the gate of the walled garden, unlike Grandma Kelvin and Yazz, who were running down to the gate. Fred followed slowly behind them. Witch Matilda told them to be quick as there wasn't any time to waste. As Witch Matilda opened the heavy wooden door, the brightness of the garden seemed to burst out through the door. I felt so alive. I looked round at Grandma, and she was glowing. Yazz was as excited as me. Kelvin wasn't saying anything. He looked as if he were in deep thought. This moment was a chance in a lifetime, and we all knew it. I felt very proud of Grandma.

Witch Matilda led us through the garden. 'Please do not set foot off the purple path,' she instructed.

The garden was breath-taking at every turn. The apples were so shiny, the flowers so bright. The purple path was glowing, and the smell was delicious. The walled garden was bursting with life. Butterflies – thousands of them. It was as if they loved Yazz because they were floating around her, beautiful butterflies of all colours. It just so magical, and Yazz was loving the attention. The greenhouse was from the Victorian era and looked brand new. Winston must have to spend hours every year keeping the glass ... immaculate was the only word that came to mind. I could see the reddest tomatoes growing in the greenhouse, like little lightbulbs. Fred couldn't get over the flowers and how magnificent they looked and smelt – flowers of every colour you could imagine. The vegetable patch was perfectly laid out, with rhubarb, and every kind of root vegetable – beetroot, carrots, parsnips, swede, potatoes, just about everything. Then we came across the orchard, with its rows of trees: apple, pear, plum, cherry, lemons, and grape vines. I never realised we ate so much. Grandma was amazed at the water feature, and the walled garden also had its own little river network – the water was so clear. There were also little footbridges and waterfalls and fountains. The soothing sound of the water flowing was magical.

On the far side of the walled garden there were built-in wood-burning fires, and as we got nearer you could feel the warmth. I could see that this was for the tropical plants: coconut, star fruit, mango, pineapple, persimmon, and some others that I had never seen before. The smell of the fresh herbs was so powerful.

In the centre of the garden was a clock tower. As well as the time, it also showed the date. Kelvin was very impressed with the clock. The clock tower was gold with lights shining down. It was very impressive to look at. Never in your wildest dreams could you ever have imagined how beautiful and wonderful this garden was. Witch Matilda urged us to be quick. 'There is no time to waste!' she urged us. In a way, it was such a shame that we didn't have more time to spend looking around the garden. I thought to myself how the gardener – no, I most address him by his name – Winston had made a perfect job of looking after this magnificent, splendid garden.

Then we reached the secret gate, which looked like the entrance gate, except much larger. There was also a staircase leading up to it. I looked over at Kelvin. He was the first one at the top of the staircase, still very confident and determined to what he could to help.

Witch Matilda and Kelvin were standing at the top of the staircase. 'Okay, are you all ready?' asked Witch Matilda. 'The time on the gate is still set on exactly the same time when the children went through, so once we go in, we should be in exactly the same place at the same time, if we are very lucky.' We all nodded hard. 'There is something else I need to tell you all,' she continued. 'I will only be visible to you five. Nobody else will be able to see me. We must not forget that much time has passed, so once we are on the other side, the top of the gate should display the time, date and year at which we arrived. Fingers crossed it will be the same.' We all looked very anxious. Even Witch Matilda seemed unsure if we were doing the right thing, and I sensed much uncertainty.

Witch Matilda could see that we were all anxious. She said, 'Daisy has brought us all here. We now must try and find the answers.'

By then, we had all gathered at the top of the staircase. Fred looked at the top of the gate and date read it out: 'May 1907. That's over a hundred year ago! This should be very interesting.'

Witch Matilda told Kelvin, 'You must walk through first. Then, set your watch when I give you the signal, and we must all hold hands very tight so that we walk through together. Our link must not be broken. Now, are we ready?'

None of us was ready, but we couldn't back out now. Our lives depended on this moment. I remembered what Grandma had said: if we don't try, how can we live the rest of our lives knowing and not doing anything about it? The anticipation of going through the secret gate was building amongst us, and I wondered what the entrance was going to entail. Would there be an almighty blast of wind swirling around us? Would I feel a falling sensation? Who knows? So, I shouted out, 'Let's go!'

Witch Matilda opened the gate. It made the loudest screech and we could see the gate was hard to open. Kelvin helped Witch Matilda push the gate open.

Because he was the first the walk through, Kelvin paused for a split second and reminded us all of the time: 18.12. But then Kelvin shouted, 'Stop! Stop!'

Now we all felt afraid. Grandma said softly, 'What's the matter, Kelvin?'

'We must not walk through until 18.15 so that our return will be exactly at 06.15. It's easier to remember.'

We all took a deep breath let out a sigh of relief. Then, at exactly 18.15, we all walked through. Kelvin timed us, and it took us 2.15 seconds precisely. There wasn't a gust of wind; in fact, there was nothing – complete silence. We were all looking at each other, waiting for something to happen, but nothing did. And then we heard the almighty bang of the gate closing. As we turned back to make sure we were all through, I noticed the date at the top of the door: May 1931. I did a quick sum in my head. That would mean the children were aged thirty-one and thirty-three – not children any more. We all looked around, trying to take in our surroundings and work out where we were.

Witch Matilda said, 'This is where the children would have started.'

As we were all looking around, we could see we were in the backstage area of a theatre. It all felt very old and dark. I noticed the ropes hanging down from the roof as I looked up. It made me feel disoriented, somewhat dizzy, because the building was so tall. There were lots of very large panels hanging on the rope.

Grandma could see that I was looking up. She told me, 'That is the scenery, hanging from the roof. Each panel is a different scene.'

'Okay,' said Witch Matilda. We don't have much time to find the missing children.'

I replied, 'They aren't children.'

'Now, what do you mean?' said Yazz.

'Look at the date above the door – 1931. That makes the daughters thirty-one and thirty-three.'

Grandma replied, 'This is going to be very difficult.'

Witch Matilda replied, 'We cannot do anything about that. We can only do our best now.'

'We're not dressed for 1931. We're going to stand out like sore thumbs,' said Fred.

Witch Matilda said, 'That's a good thing, because people will be intrigued by you, and they will want to know what you're doing here. That way, you can start asking around straight away.'

'Good idea,' said Fred, 'We haven't any time to waste.'

Nobody had noticed until then that Kelvin was sitting on the floor. 'I don't like in here,' he said. He was counting, rocking back and forth. Grandma and Fred picked Kelvin up and tried to calm him down. Grandma reminded Kelvin that we all had a job to do, and to remember he was keeping the time.

I was looking around and finally I could see the theatre's exit, which was open. Just then, a tall, grey-haired, well-spoken man came walking towards us.

He shouted, 'Can I help you? What are you doing in here?' As he got nearer, he said, 'You shouldn't be in here. What are you doing in here?'

Grandma said, 'Ah well, oh dear.'

Witch Matilda whispered in Grandma's ear, 'Don't hesitate, Daisy. Speak up. Remember, we need to get back in here to return home.'

'Yes, yes, of course, you're right,' Grandma whispered back. Then Grandma's voice got very stern as she addressed the man. 'Good afternoon, sir. The door was open, so we wanted to come in and have a look around. You see, we are looking for the two little girls that went missing a long time ago, and we were told that this was where they entered from another time, and we are trying to find them.'

The man replied with a worried look on his face, 'Good afternoon, I'm Arthur.'

'I'm Daisy, this is my friend Fred, and these are my grandchildren Kelvin, Yazz and Max.'

'Very nice to meet all of you. Just wait there, and I will put on some lights.' When the lights came on, I noticed the theatre was very grand. I saw it was called the Royal Electric Theatre.

Arthur returned and asked, 'Did you mention two little girls?'

'Yes,' replied Grandma.

Arthur said, 'There was once a story going around about two little girls, but it was before my time at the Royal, and if I'm honest I thought the story was just made up to create interest around the theatre, get people talking, you know what I mean? Like something of a publicity stunt. Never in my wildest dreams did I ever imagine there was any truth in the story. Daisy, please do tell.'

'Yes, we have just entered through that door, to be honest,' Grandma said, and pointed to the door, 'and we have come from the year 2017.'

Arthur asked, 'Is 2017 a good year?'

'It will be if we find the lost children.'

'Yes, of course. How did the children get here?'

'They came through the secret gate, which is within our walled garden. The children had gone before anybody realised, and because they were so young, they didn't know how to return. They missed their timeslot. We only have twelve hours to find them before we have to return, otherwise we will also be lost in time, the same as the children.'

Arthur asked, 'Will you need to return through the same door?'

'Yes,' replied Fred. 'Will you help us to get back in, if that's okay?'

'Yes that'll be okay,' said Arthur, 'and I think you should speak to Mrs Dawson.'

'Who is Mrs Dawson?' asked Grandma.

'Mrs Dawson is the owner, and she will probably know more about the children.'

'Is Mrs Dawson here now?' asked Fred.

'No, she is at home, but I could call her, and I'm sure she would be happy to help you. What time must you leave?'

Kelvin spoke up. 'I'm the timekeeper, and we must leave here by 6.15 p.m. your time, which is 06.15 a.m. for us.' Kelvin went on to explain that he keeps time all around the world. Arthur was very impressed by this and kept asking Kelvin the time in different places in the world.

Grandma said, 'Okay, we have been here twenty minutes already, so—'

'Grandma, you're wrong,' Kelvin interrupted. 'We have been here twenty-four minutes and thirty-two, thirty-three, thirty-four seconds precisely.' Kelvin was keeping the time

116

of every second, which was a good idea as we couldn't afford to waste any time.

'We need to start looking around and trying to speak to people,' said Fred.

Arthur asked, 'Are you going outside?'

'Yes,' said Grandma. 'But why do you ask?'

'Because you're not going to fit in here with those clothes. Remember, you have arrived in 1931, and please excuse me, but that dress code will not work here.'

Yazz quickly replied, 'We don't have any other clothes.'

Arthur thought for a moment and said, 'Follow me. You see, my job in the theatre is in the dressing room, so I can lend you some clothes, but I must have them back before you return, otherwise Mrs Dawson will have my head on the block.'

I looked at Yazz and said under my breath, 'Head on the block? What is he on about, Yazz?'

Yazz shrugged her shoulders. 'No idea.'

Fred overheard us and said, 'Head on the block means, chop off your head, like in medieval times.'

I looked at Yazz and said, 'If Mrs Dawson is carrying an axe, I'm off.'

Yazz laughed. 'Off? Where to?'

Arthur was very good at his job. With one glance, he knew our sizes and just how to dress us, and what clothes suited us best. Grandma was first, and as quick as lightning, she had been transformed into a 1930s lady with a navy blue dress edged with cream satin and a cream satin belt. The bottom of the dress was heavily pleated, and the fabric was a cotton drill. Grandma looked so nice. Yazz said, 'Grandma, you look beautiful.' Grandma's face lit up.

Yazz insisted it be her turn next. Arthur picked the same

dress as Grandma's, only it was cream, and edged with navy blue. By then, Fred had found himself a grey suit to put on, and Arthur had given his approval. And now it was my turn. Arthur picked short trousers, a cream shirt with a tank of all colours, a blazer and a flat cap. I didn't much like what I was wearing, but there wasn't any time for moaning. Witch Matilda stood in complete silence and watched our every move. She wasn't pleased that we were changing our clothes, and she had advised against it, but Grandma had argued that she thought we needed to, to avoid wasting time by having to explain to everybody why we looked different. Arthur had no idea Witch Matilda was here, of course. I wondered to myself what he would think if he could see her. Would he believe she was a witch, or would he think she was just someone dressed up, pretending to be a witch? And how would we explain the journey we had all made? Arthur would never believe that. Only a couple of hours ago, we were listening to a ludicrous greedy old man, and before that, we were following an elephant to a little ferry boat. This day will be unforgettable, that was for sure.

Arthur pointed at Kelvin and said, 'Okay, young man, it's your turn.'

Nobody had noticed Kelvin was sitting in the corner again, not saying anything, just looking at his watch and rocking back and forth.

Grandma went straight over to Kelvin. Arthur asked, 'Is he okay?'

Kelvin told Grandma that he wasn't changing his clothes.

Grandma explained to Arthur that Kelvin was autistic, but of course, 1931 autism wasn't much known about, so Arthur had no idea what Grandma was talking about.

Grandma looked at Arthur and realised she had to change her approach. 'Sorry, in layman's terms, it's what's known as a social disorder.'

Still looking puzzled, Arthur said, 'I'm sorry, I don't understand.'

Grandma took a deep breath, her patience wearing thin, and said, 'I'm really sorry, I don't have time much time to explain. Kelvin doesn't like much social contact, especially with people he doesn't know, and he finds new things hard sometimes. Kelvin will not change his clothes.'

Arthur replied, 'But he will stand out.

Kelvin looked straight at Arthur and said, 'I'm not changing. I like my own clothes.'

Arthur looked slightly shocked and disappointed. He really enjoyed dressing us up, and he was good at his job.

Yazz said to Arthur, 'You have done a great job. We all look fabulous. Kelvin only likes what he likes. He really doesn't wish to upset you.'

Arthur shrugged his shoulders with a small smile and replied, 'Okay.'

We all looked very 1930s. Kelvin was very upset and told us all, 'We have spent far too much time – fifty-three minutes twenty-one seconds to be precise, and now we need to get moving if we are going to find the children. We only have eleven hours, seven minutes, thirty-six seconds. Now, please can we get moving!' Kelvin seemed to be taking control of the situation.

Grandma said, 'You're right, Kelvin. We need to get on with the job we have come here to do.' Then Grandma turned to Arthur. 'Thank you for all your help. Can we rely on you to be here when we return?'

Arthur replied with a smile, 'Yes, of course. But you're not going home until all my clothes are all returned.'

'Have you got any advice for us before we go on our search?' I asked Arthur.

Arthur thought for a moment and said, 'Yes, make your way to the Anchor Hotel. Not much gets past the owner of the Anchor. He knows everything that goes on in Cradley Heath.'

Grandma looked at Arthur a bit bewildered, and Fred said, 'Did you say Cradley Heath?'

'Yes,' said Arthur, 'Cradley Heath. Why?'

We all looked at each other. Yazz said, 'Cradley Heath – is that the name of this area?'

'Yes,' said Arthur. He looked at us all and said, 'You have no idea where you are, do you?'

'No,' said Grandma.

Witch Matilda walked over to Daisy and whispered, 'You haven't put enough thought into any of this, have you, Daisy?'

Grandma put her head down and covered her face with her hands and quietly replied, 'No, I guess not. Nowhere near enough thought. What was I thinking?'

Witch Matilda replied, 'Definitely not. The consequences of your actions.'

Daisy went red and said, 'Yes, yes, I know this could all be one big mistake.'

Arthur asked, 'Are you taking to me?'

'No, sorry, just talking to myself. The first sign of going senile.'

Arthur looked straight at Grandma and said, 'Oh no.' We all looked at Arthur, and then he added, 'Not much hope for me, then. I'm always talking to myself!'

We started to laugh. Kelvin started to pace the floor very impatiently, grumbling, 'I really think we should make a move now.'

'Yes you're right,' said Fred. 'This is all taking far too long.'

'How do we get to the Anchor Hotel from here?' asked Yazz.

'That there is the stage door, which leads out to Bank Street, so out the door, turn left at the top of Bank Street, turn right onto the High Street. At the end of the High Street, you come to Five Ways. Take your first right, and the Anchor Hotel is just twenty yards up, on your left. The landlord is very nice. If anybody can help you, he can. Not much happens in Cradley Heath without his knowledge.'

As we walked out of the theatre, an overwhelming feeling came over me. I felt myself taking a deep breath I realised I was walking into the unknown. I didn't say anything to the others, but as I looked round at them, I could see by the look on their faces that they were thinking the same thing. I knew my Grandma always means well, and she is only trying to do the right thing. I had to think about what I had learnt from this at this moment, that some things are best left in peace. Another thought entered my head then: the lost children, who were grown women with hopefully children of their own – how would this affect them, if we could find them? That question was yet to be answered.

As we stepped out onto the footpath the first thing we noticed was a loud banging noise. The noise was echoing all around and seemed to be bouncing off the buildings around us, and no matter which way you turned it was still as loud. Grandma turned back and asked Arthur, 'What is that noise, and where is it coming from?'

'That is the hammers makings the chains.'

Just then, there was an even louder noise, causing Kelvin to cover his ears with his hands.

Arthur smiled and said, 'Don't worry, that's the chain. After the chain has been made, they tip the bucket to pour the chain out so they can make the next chain.' Arthur looked at Grandma. 'You have no idea where you are, do you?'

Grandma shook her head with an anxious look on her face.

Arthur asked Grandma, 'Where do you live?'

'In a little village outside Cambridge.'

Arthur smiled and said, 'That explains the look of dismay on your faces. You are in the heart of the industrial Midlands, the engine room of Great Britain. *Cambridge* Cambridgeshire is quite a contrast to the *Black Country* Cambridgeshire which sits in East Anglia, known as the bread basket of the UK,' said Fred.

Yazz said, 'Black Country? But you said we were in Cradley Heath!'

'Yes, that's right, we are in Cradley Heath. Cradley Heath is just one of many places that make up the district of the Black Country. Something else I need tell you – the accent and dialect are slightly different to Cambridge, so when you are spoken to, listen carefully.'

'Okay,' replied Grandma.

'I'm going to be here most of the day, so if you get stuck I will come and help you. In the meantime, when Mrs Dawson returns, I will ask her what she knows of the children, in case you don't get to meet the landlord and more information is needed.'

Fred said, 'Let's get moving and see what we can find out.'

We walked up Bank Street, and at the junction with the High Street we turned right, as Arthur had told us. The High Street was very busy, and there were lots of people on both sides, the footpaths packed with shoppers. Everybody looked very smart. It was a good job Arthur had insisted we change our clothes.

As we walked down towards the Five Ways junction, I found myself looking in the shop windows. For the first time in my life, I was window-shopping, an expression I'd heard Grandma and Mum use many times but hadn't really understood what they were talking about. I noticed there was a shoe repair shop, a baker, greengrocer, dressmaker. The shop next to the dress makers was the clothes repair and alterations shop, and next was the jewellery shop that also did watch repairs, then the butcher, and the fishmonger. There was a shop for everything, and the shops stretched all the way down to the Five Ways junction on both sides of the road. There was a newsagent, stationery shop, sweet shop, gift shop, several women's clothes shops and men's clothes shops, shoe shops, general stores, sewing shop, carpet shop, curtain shop, fabric shop, a wool shop (with hundreds of knitting needles displayed in the window), book shop, several banks, a general post office, an ironmonger, there was a shop for everything. I also noticed that the shops were busy, and the people working in the shops all looked happy, chatting away. I noticed everybody coming out of the shop had a satisfying look on their faces, and a smile. There were two indoor markets halls. The atmosphere in the High Street felt warm, very nice and content.

Then I realised something: this must have been life before the giant supermarkets arrived. I looked round, and Grandma, Fred, Yazz and even Kelvin were walking slowly and looking in all the shop windows as they passed. It had to be said that this was a nice way to shop – a different experience. For the first few minutes, we had all forgotten what we were looking for.

Just before we reached the top of the High Street, on the opposite side of the road was a shop called Woolworths. Grandma and Fred were delighted to see this shop and had a look of excitement on their faces.

I asked Grandma, 'Do you know the people who own that shop?'

Grandma smiled and shook her head and said, 'No, I just remember shopping in Woolworths. It was a really nice shop and I miss being able to shop there.'

'Are you sad, Grandma?' asked Kelvin.

'Yes, I'm very sad to see Woolworths again. Grandad Jim loved Woolworths. In fact, it was the only shop he liked to look round.'

Whilst we were all standing on the opposite side of the street admiring Woolworths, someone decided to have a chat to Kelvin. Luckily, Witch Matilda had noticed this and so she stood at Kelvin's side. A young lad was asking Kelvin where he'd bought his shoes from.

Witch Matilda carefully told Kelvin to tell the young lad that the shoes were a present from America.

Fred said to Grandma, 'I think that's a very wise answer.'

Thankfully, Kelvin was very calm and answered politely. normally he would walk away and not answer. We were all very proud of Kelvin. When the young lad spoke, as Arthur had said, he sounded much different to us, and the dialect was also slightly different. Although the accent sounded different to anything that I had heard before, it somehow came across as very sincere and friendly when the young lad spoke. I felt like I was with an old friend, even though I didn't know him.

After Grandma and Fred had finished admiring Woolworths, we all turned round, and the young lad asked, 'Yam all together?'

Yazz replied, 'Yes.'

'I've never seen yo round here before.'

'No, we are not from round here. We are from Cambridgeshire. My name is Yazz.'

'It's very nice to meet yo, Yazz. My name is Jack. Am this your family?'

'Yes,' replied Yazz. 'Grandma, Daisy, Fred, and my two brothers Kelvin and Max.'

Jack replied, as he lifted his flat cap, 'Very nice to meet yo all. What do yo think of our little town?'

'Very nice,' replied Fred. 'You have everything you could ever wish to buy in this High Street. It's very pleasant.'

'Yo like it here, then?'

Grandma said, 'Up to now, yes.'

Jack replied, 'I've heard Cambridge am lovely. Ar would like to go there someday, but ar will need a bike because the town am full of bikes, am that correct?'

'Yes,' said Yazz.

Jack said, 'I've heard it's worth a visit just to study the architecture of the buildings. People say it's beautiful.'

Fred replied, 'It is a very beautiful town, it has to be said, and definitely worth a visit.'

Jack said, 'Ar better let yo bostin people get on with your day. Ar could talk all day. Ar hope yo enjoy your time in Cradley Heath.'

Grandma said, I'm sure we will, and it's been a pleasure to meet you, Jack. I will say good day to you.'

Jack replied, 'Tarar-a-bit' and off he went.

'He seemed a nice young lad,' said Grandma.

'Yes,' replied Fred. 'Very polite.'

'Arthur was right. The dialect is different. "Tarar-a-bit" must mean goodbye.'

'Yes,' said Fred. It's goodbye, because as he said it, he raised his hand and waved at the same time.'

Yazz said, 'Bostin – I think that means good.'

'Yes,' said Grandma, 'because when he used the word "bostin" he smiled politely.'

I said, 'I like this dialect. It feels friendly.'

We carried on up towards Five Ways. Once we reached the junction, we could see why it was called Five Ways: traffic was coming in all five directions. Luckily, it wasn't all cars: there were plenty of horses and carts. Witch Matilda was following us, not saying anything – although of course she did help Kelvin out with the young lad. I still felt fascinated by Witch Matilda. I wished everybody could see her as we could. They would think the Queen had arrived and that we were her family.

As we got to the top of the High Street, Kelvin said, 'It's taken far too long to walk that distance up the High Street. We have now been here one hour, forty-seven minutes, thirteen seconds.'

Grandma replied, 'Try not to worry, Kelvin. We can only do our best. If we don't find the children, that's how it's meant to be, and there isn't anything we can do about that.'

At Five Ways we turned sharp right onto St Anne's Road, and just there on the left-hand side was the Anchor Hotel. Witch Matilda was now using her broomstick, and as we all looked at the Anchor, she was standing on the roof looking down at us all. I wondered to myself what was she doing up there, but as I looked up at her in that beautiful dress, I thought how at least she wasn't going to

126

get dirty up there. It has to be said that the roads are very dirty in this day and age. I looked around to make sure nobody could see, then waved up to her. She smiled and nodded her head. We crossed the road and walked down to the Anchor. The name of the hotel bar's landlord was above the door: William Thomas Hackman. Grandma and Fred thought it best if Kelvin, Yazz and I waited outside, as it was a bar. Standing looking at the front of the Anchor, I noticed a little sign that read *Hotel*, with an arrow pointing to the side of the building. I suggested that we go round to the side, as that part was the hotel.

'Good idea,' said Grandma.

We made our way round to the side door, but it was locked, so Fred knocked on the door. Within a few minutes, a dark-haired lady opened the door and looked at all five of us and said, 'Sorry, we am full tonight.' Then the lady quickly shut the door.

We all looked at each other, a bit bewildered. Fred shook his head in disbelief and knocked again.

We all heard her stamp her foot, and then she shouted out loud 'We'm full! Don't yo understand?'

Fred shouted back, 'We're not looking for a room. We would like to speak to Mr Hackman.'

'He's busy. Come back later.'

Grandma was getting very upset, and still shouting through the door she replied, 'We can't come back later. We don't have much time.'

With that the door opened again the same lady said, 'What do yo want to speak to Mr Hackman about?'

'We are looking for two little girls that were lost many years ago, and we have been told to asked at the Anchor Hotel because anything that happens in Cradley Heath is most probably talked about here.'

The dark-haired lady said, 'Ar don't have any idea want yo am talking about, but ar will ask Mr Hackman to come straight away.'

Grandma replied, 'Much appreciated.'

The dark-haired lady closed the door, and we could hear her walking upstairs. Within a few minutes the door opened again and this time it was Mr Hackman. He was a smart, regular-build fellow with short brown hair.

'Good afternoon. I'm Mr Hackman, the licence holder of this establishment. How can ar help yo?'

Fred replied, 'It has been brought to our attention that many years ago two little girls got lost in Cradley Heath, and we wondered if you know anything about this?'

Mr Hackman had a look of shock, which quickly turned to relief. He stood for a few seconds and looked at us all and said, 'You're not from round here, am yo?'

Fred replied, 'No.'

'What do yo know of the two little girls?'

Grandma said, 'We know they are lost in time. We know where they come from, and we know their father.'

If you know so much, why has it taken yo so long to come and look for them?'

Grandma replied, 'It's a very long story and we don't have much time.'

Mr Hackman said, 'Yo'd better come inside.'

As we walked through the door there was a terrible smell. I asked Fred, 'What's that smell?'

'Spilt beer and tobacco.'

Mr Hackman said, 'Come in, sit down.' He had taken us to the back, which was nicely decorated and the smell wasn't so strong there.

Mr Hackman said, 'Now, who am yo? Tell me your names. I'm William.'

Fred replied, 'I'm Fred, and this is my good friend Daisy, and her grandchildren – Yazz, Kelvin and Max.'

Mr Hackman replied, 'It's very nice to meet yo all.'

Kelvin placed himself in the corner. I sensed this was becoming too much for him, so Yazz and I went and sat with him. Kelvin whispered to us that this was all taking far too long.

Yazz said, 'Kelvin, it'll be okay. Don't worry.'

Kelvin replied, 'But what if we miss our timeslot and we're trapped here?'

I had never even considered that. My only thoughts were about the lost children. I could not imagine being lost in time; the difference between 1931 and 2017 is a world apart. Then I thought, how did the girls manage? They must have been terrified. That thought had never entered my head before, and then I remembered what Witch Matilda had said. The word she had used so many times: consequences. Always remember they will be consequences.

Mr Hackman said, 'It's clear to me listening to yo that yo am here with good intentions. Most people who came here looking for the girls only wanted to claim them as their own.'

Daisy said, 'Yes, Mr Hackman. Our intentions are very good. You see, their father, Winston, has waited every day since the children went through the secret gate in the walled garden for them to return, and now he is very old. It has taken a lifetime for me to realise that the missing children belong to Winston because Winston is a very secret man and never burdens others with his problems.'

Mr Hackman said, 'The first thing ar need to tell yo am that my sister had a lot of involvement with the two little girls. Her looked after them whilst the police and other authorities tried to find the parents. My sister Ada already had five children of her own – three girls and two boys. I don't know how her managed to keep things together, but our Ada did, and her never let Flora and Stella out of sight.'

'Did your Ada have a husband?' asked Grandma.

'Arr Ada had a bostin husband – Sammy – and he had bostin job. He was the foreman at Dudley and Dowell. Ar Ada had two terraced houses, and Sammy made them into one, so they had plenty of room. Ar Ada never had to go to work, Sammy made sure of that.'

'Did Flora and Stella stay with your Ada indefinitely?' asked Grandma.

'No, but they did stay with ar Ada for about six months, until they were properly placed, and that took a lot of working out because nobody really knew where they had come from.'

'Were the police involved?' asked Fred.

'Arr, the police were involved from the start. Ar Ada spotted the girls up the High Street, wandering around, crying. Ar Ada told us her knew they weren't from around here. Ar Ada thought they were from a wealthy family because of the way they were dressed. Ar Ada said they looked very smart, so ar Ada sent for the police straight away.'

'Didn't the police take them away?' asked Fred.

'No. The police asked ar Ada if her could take them in until the parents could be found. Well, the police knew they would be safe at ar Ada's house. Her loved kids. I do believe ar Ada would have loved to have kept Flora and Stella, but seven children was too much to look after, and her couldn't afford to pay for any help.'

Grandma asked, are Flora and Stella safe and well?'

'Arr, Flora's husband has the shoe repair shop in the High Street. Ar spoke to him last week.'

'Are both women in this area?'

'Arr, both Flora and Stella live local. Please tell me about Flora.'

'Her's tall with an average build. Flora works in the children's home for orphaned children. Flora has two sons. Jack's ten, the oldest and then there's Winston, who's six. Flora am very well known and very well-liked in Cradley Heath. Flora also has the best garden in Cradley Heath, which her am very proud of.'

'Flora sounds much like her father,' said Daisy, and as for Jack, I think we might have just met in the High Street.'

'Possibly. Jack's always up the High Street. Smart-looking young lad.'

'Yes, very polite.'

'That'll be Jack. He doesn't miss anything or anybody.'

'What about Winston?' asked Yazz.

'Winston am quite a young lad, so yo don't see that one very much, and when yo do he's always with his mother.'

Fred asked, 'Can you tell us anything about Stella?'

'Stella's husband is a travelling showman. After growing up on the fairground her married a showman from another funfair family. Stella once told our Ada her loved living in a caravan. Her husband owns a little funfair.' Then Mr Hackman paused. I looked up at him saw he was looking at Grandma and Fred. 'Forgive me for saying, but yo both look surprised.'

Grandma, stumbling on her words, said, 'Oh, well, um, you see, that wasn't what I was expecting you to say. Sorry if I look surprised.'

I also noticed Grandma and Fred looked surprised, but I

couldn't understand why. It was as if Mr Hackman had said something to offend Grandma and Fred. William had the same surprised look on his face.

Grandma, looking slightly puzzled, asked Mr Hackman, 'Did you say the girls grew up on a funfair?'

I could see Mr Hackman was getting annoyed with Grandma. 'Arr. Am there something wrong with that?'

Grandma quickly replied, 'No, of course not. I'm sure they had a wonderful life.'

In an angry tone of voice, Mr Hackman said, 'They did. Both Flora and Stella never wanted for anything. Brilliant upbringing they had.' Mr Hackman went on, 'Mr and Mrs Bones am genuinely lovely people. As ar told yo, our Ada took both girls in. After all the investigations and many searches, everybody involved needed to accept that the girls were lost and they had no way of getting them home. Can yo imagine how upsetting that was for Flora and Stella? So, our Ada looked after them both, like they were her very own children until a suitable home could be found. The next problem came when they were both put up for adoption, and nobody would adopt both girls, and Ada refused to separate them. Our Ada promised the girls they would not be separated, and that was a promise our Ada was going to keep. Our Ada told me herself her was going to adopt them both so they wouldn't be separated if needs be. Our Ada was bostin friends with Mrs Bones. Her had children of her own but they were grown up. Mrs Bones offered to take both girls on if no suitable home could be found, so after six months, when it was established that no suitable home could be found, Mr and Mrs Bones went to see our Ada and told her the offer still stood. The next problem was the authorities, who were concerned about Mr and Mrs Bones' lifestyle of travelling around. If they adopted the girls, would they be able to attend school full time? And being part of the funfair, wouldn't that be a problem? Mrs Bones told the authorities her could send them to a full-time boarding school if education was going to be a problem. The girls were desperate to stay together, and our Ada had promised they would not be separated. It turned out that when the authorities investigated, Mr and Mrs Bones were quite wealthy. Not only did they own a funfair, but it came to light that they were also property and landowners as well. So in fact, Mr and Mrs Bones were perfectly positioned to adopted both Flora and Stella. It was agreed between our Ada, Mrs Bones and the authorities that they would work together to ensure the girls' educational needs and anything else would be met without fail, They had a very good upbringing, thanks to our Ada and Mr and Mrs Bones. It was also agreed that two weekends in every month they would visit our Ada. Her acted like a kind of grandma figure, and our Ada had kids the same age, so the arrangement worked perfectly.

Grandma said, 'Let me sum up the situation. Both Flora and Stella are safe and well, married with children?'

'Arr. Like I said, Flora has two boys – Jack and Winston. And Stella has two girls, named Ada, after our Ada, and Flora, after her sister.'

Grandma went on. 'Flora married a shoe repair man, and Stella married a travelling showman, and both girls grew up on the funfair after being adopted by Mr and Mrs Bones, which was supported by your sister, Ada.'

Mr Hackman replied, 'Yes, and they am both very happy.'

Daisy looked at Fred with a look of dismay on her face and said, 'What now?'

Witch Matilda had been hovering around the room, listening to every word.

Mr Hackman said, 'If yo have come here to take Flora and Stella home, ar think yo am wasting your time.'

Daisy said, 'Yes, I can see that now.'

Mr Hackman said, 'I'm going to leave yo alone a moment whilst ar get yo all something to eat. Will fish and chips be alright?'

Fred smiled and said, 'Some things never change. Fish and chips would be lovely.'

Mr Hackman left the room, and there was an unpleasant silence while we all sat looking at each other. I could see Grandma was looking very frustrated. I felt slightly sorry for her because I know she was only been trying to do a good deed.

Finally, the silence was broken when Witch Matilda said, 'Daisy, I know that you have only come all this way to be kind, and if you decide to turn around and go home, nobody would think any less of you.'

Then Kelvin said loudly, 'We have been here three hours, eighteen minutes and twenty-six seconds.' Kelvin was still obviously really annoyed with how long everything was taking.

Witch Matilda replied, 'Kelvin, you are doing a very good job and so are Daisy and Fred. It is most important that we find out as much information as possible. The more information we have, the more time we can save. I understand it's difficult for you, but please try and be patient.'

Grandma looked at Witch Matilda and whispered, 'Thank you.' I saw how she still had a look of dismay on her face. She added, 'We have to think very carefully about our next move. We don't know Mr Hackman. However, listening to all the information he has given, it sounds like Flora and Stella have had a good childhood and have both done well for themselves. The question is do we check to make sure what Mr Hackman has told us is true, and if so should we go home and say no more about what we have done, or go and meet Flora and Stella and be totally honest and tell them why we have come here?'

Witch Matilda said, 'You have reached a crossroad. Where you go from here could work out to be the best thing you have ever done or the worst thing you have ever done. The next decision is the hardest one yet. The consequences could be very tough – too tough live with.'

Grandma replied, 'Thank you for reminding me about the consequences, Witch Matilda. I do understand now that what I'm doing might not be the best thing, and definitely not my best idea.'

Grandma sat in silence for a moment, and then after a few minutes said with a definite tone of voice, 'Once I realised that the lost children could be Winston's, I knew I needed to find out. When my son Tom was born, I spent much of my time wondering to myself what he would look like when he became an adult and which member of our family he would look like. My son is now forty-nine years of age, and I still look with wonder. With all that in mind, I imagine that Winston must feel the same, exactly the same, only he has the uncertainty of not knowing if Flora and Stella are even alive. I believe I have made the best decision, so I'm ready to face the consequences and any difficulties that may occur.'

Witch Matilda replied, 'I will do what I can to help you.'

Mr Hackman returned with fish and chips for everyone. We were all very pleased. Our day had been so busy that we had forgotten about eating. We all unwrapped the paper – Mr Hackman included – and then the whole room filled with the delicious smell, which I noticed was much different to our fish and chips back home.

Mr Hackman informed us, 'These am the best fish and chips because they am cooked in dripping.' I thought to myself, that's why they smell so good and taste so much nicer. As I was eating, I thought to myself, how are we going to pay for our fish and chips? Even if Grandma has cash, I'm sure it's not the same kind as in 1931. We had pounds and pence, but in 1931 we would need a shilling or half a crown, and I didn't even know what they looked like. Hopefully, Mr Hackman would treat us. Fingers crossed.

The room went completely silent for about fifteen minutes whilst everybody was eating, and then the silence was broken when in walked the lady with the dark hair that answered the door. She had a tray with cups of tea for everyone. She put the tray down without saying a word, nodded and left the room.

After all the tea was gone, Mr Hackman asked Grandma, 'What am yo going to do now? Because if I'm honest, if ar can be frank, yo might be better off going home and forgetting all this. Flora and Stella am very happy. Why put them through any upheaval?'

Grandma turned to Mr Hackman. 'I understand what you are saying, and to a degree you're right. However, we have come from a much smaller world than you are living in now, a world where communication around the entire world is so easy, with no barriers to overcome. Flora and Stella's father, Winston, is very old, I'm sad to say. He's probably not got much more time left on this planet. Every day Winston spends most of his time working in the walled garden and we have only just learnt why. We always knew that two children got lost in the walled garden and we all thought that the story was older than our village, but now we know otherwise. Winston has spent most of his life in the walled garden, praying one day Flora and Stella will return. When I started this journey, I believed I was doing the right thing, but if I'm honest I've had many doubts along the way. However, the burning desire inside that I'm doing the right thing has kept me going. And I have learnt that the consequences of my actions may not be the end result that we have been looking for.'

Mr Hackman stood up and said, 'Daisy, yo am a very brave woman.'

Grandma had a look of relief on her face because she had come to learn that Mr Hackman was very protective of Flora and Stella.

Fred asked Mr Hackman, 'Do you think it would be possible if we could meet your sister Ada?'

A darkness came over Mr Hackman's face, like someone had just pulled the blinds down. He had gone very pale. He dropped his head down, took a deep breath and said in a soft tone of voice, 'Ar wish ar could take yo see to our Ada, but her passed away just over two years ago. Heart attack.'

Fred said, 'We are very sad to hear this. Your Ada sounds like a great lady.'

I looked over at Grandma, and I could see her eyes filling with tears, though she never said anything.

Mr Hackman said, 'Arr, our Ada was the heart and soul of Cradley Heath. Her family will never get over their loss. Luckily enough, all her children am old enough to take care of themselves now. But Sammy, he will never but the same.'

Then the room went silent again, and after what seemed a never-ending silence, Grandma said, 'I'm sorry about your Ada. Now I understand why you are so protective of Flora and Stella.'

Arr, our Ada would have wanted someone to keep their best interests at heart.'

Fred asked Mr Hackman, 'Do you think we could meet Flora and Stella?'

Mr Hackman said, 'Do yo think that's the best idea? My honest opinion am think yo getting into hot water. What if your visit goes wrong?'

Witch Matilda walked over to Daisy and said, 'Mr Hackman seems very reluctant to allow you to visit Flora and Stella, so ask him what Ada would think of this situation.'

'Yes, Mr Hackman, I fully understand your concerns, but I've thought of nothing else since we started this journey, and we only have one chance, and I'm sure that Flora and Stella will understand our situation, and I think it's safe to say that your Ada would have loved to have made contact with Flora and Stella's parents, even if it is in this most ludicrous way.'

Mr Hackman replied, 'When yo say it like that, ar suppose yo being here, and me and my barmaid knowing that, if Flora and Stella ever found out, our Ada would turn in her grave and probably be very upset with me. If this am going to work ar think it's best yo meet Flora because her am the oldest.' Mr Hackman went into deep thought after saying this, and the uncertainty was clearly written all over his face. He stood for a while, and I could see a million thoughts were rattling around in his head. Then he said, 'What about if ar bring Flora here, because her only lives down the road.' Then, before anybody could answer, he said, 'Second thoughts, in case Flora am out, ar will goo and see Flora's husband Ivan in the shop and ar can explain what has happened here today.'

Grandma smiled and replied, 'That is a very good idea. Can we come with you?'

Mr Hackman looked surprised, and it was clear to see he didn't want Grandma to go with him. Grandma saw this too and backed off straight away, saying, 'No, actually I think it's best if we all stay together here.'

Mr Hackman was clearly relieved and wasted no time getting out of the door. He really wanted to go alone.

We were once again left alone sat hopelessly looking at each other. Then Fred stood up, never said a word and then walked out of the room. A couple of minutes later, he came back and said, 'Let's go and have a look around Cradley Heath.'

Grandma replied, 'Don't you think we'd better stay here for when Mr Hackman returns?'

'No, it's okay. I've just explained to Nel.'

'Who's Nel?' asked Yazz.

'The young lady, the one who Mr Hackman described as his barmaid. I told her that we are going out for some fresh air, and we will be back really soon.'

Kelvin stood up and said, 'We have been here four hours, eight minutes and fifty-six, fifty-seven seconds. Why is this taking so long? We only have seven hours, fifty-one minutes and three, two, one, seconds left. And I have lost track of time everywhere else.'

Grandma said, 'Don't worry about the time anywhere else, just keep tracking the time here.'

It was very clear that Kelvin was getting frustrated. Witch Matilda walked over to Kelvin and said, 'Remember what I told you, Kelvin. Information is time saved.' Kelvin nodded his head. Then we all left the back room of the Anchor Hotel.

As we stepped outside, we heard again the bang-bang,

bang-bang. The hammers were still working away, and it seemed to be louder now. We turned left and carried on walking down St Anne's Road. We were now at the back of the High Street, and all we could see were factories. As we walked past the first factories, the big steel doors were open and we could feel the heat seeping out of the doors from the open furnace, glowing red. Even outside, the heat was so intense that the men had no shirts – they were stripped down to the waist, and their bodies were black with soot, and shining with the sweat from the heat of the furnace. Nobody said anything to us, so we just stood watching. It was as if we were invisible. Whilst one team of men shovelled the coal into the furnace, another team poured the liquid iron into the moulds. Even though all the men seemed to look content at work, the inside of the factory looked like hell on earth. The noise was deafening. I thought to myself, these men work so hard in very hard conditions.

We carried on walking down St Anne's Road, and as we turned the corner, there was a little funfair. Not thinking, and feeling slightly excited, we strolled over. Kelvin was reluctant, telling us that we had been here eight hours, six minutes and twenty-two seconds. We reassured him that we would not run out of time, and Kelvin told us that he was very annoyed and didn't want to go to the fair. This was not part of the plan. Yazz managed to calm Kelvin down a bit.

There were lots of people around the funfair. Everything looked brand new and well presented. There were round game stalls, a helter-skelter, a large carousel, two small carousels and another large ride called chair-o-planes.

'Ohh, the delicious smell of toffee apples and candyfloss,'

Grandma said. 'I feel like a child again.' Then she insisted on riding on the carousel, whilst Fred was contemplating taking a ride on the helter-skelter. In our excitement, we had forgotten that we didn't have the correct money, so Grandma and Fred were so disappointed when they realised this. Yazz and I thought this was so funny.

We wandered around for while. Then Kelvin asked, 'Can we go back to Anchor Hotel now?'

Grandma said, 'Yes.'

We turned around and walked back up St Anne's Road. Grandma and Fred both looked really sad, and I felt like I was the adult and they were the children, who were sulking because they couldn't go on the rides. It was so funny.

As we got to the top of St Anne's Road, Witch Matilda was waiting for us. We felt a sense of urgency, so without saying anything, or thinking about what might await us, we quickly got back inside the Anchor Hotel. We all scuffed through the corridor that led to the back room, Grandma leading the way. That terrible smell hit me again – tobacco and spilt beer. It took your breath away.

The first person I noticed was Mr Hackman, and then there was another gentleman, then next to him was a lady, sitting on a chair. She was smartly dressed and wearing a hat. What I noticed in particular was her two-toned black and white brogue-style shoes, with rounded toes and a three-inch heel. In my opinion, they were very nice, and her dress, bag and hat all matched. The lady was smart and perfectly presented, and for some reason she reminded me of Witch Matilda. Maybe it was because she was so smartly dressed.

Witch Matilda, still looking perfect, placed herself in the corner, next to Kelvin.

We sat down and Mr Hackman said, 'I've explained to Flora and Ivan, so let me introduce yo to Flora and her husband Ivan. Ivan, Flora, this am Fred, and his bostin friend Daisy, and her grandchildren Kelvin, Yazz and Max.'

Grandma had a look of relief on her face. Then, as if someone had flicked a switch, there came a very uncomfortable silence. I hadn't expected that. Flora and Ivan knew why we were there, so why the silence? Maybe they didn't want us to be there. Maybe Flora didn't want to be reminded of her past.

Finally, the silence was broken by Mr Hackman. 'Ar think we all need a cup of tea.' With that, Mr Hackman left the room.

Grandma's look of relief had turned to a look of anxiety.

Then thankfully Ivan said, 'Have yo come far?'

Fred looked at Flora and replied, in a hesitant tone of voice, 'We have had quite a journey to get here, and I sincerely hope our journey will prove to be worth it.'

Flora looked at Fred and said, 'Why have you come here?'

Grandma replied, 'Because, thanks to Witch Matilda, and my grandson Kelvin, we were able to get here, and provided we track the time properly, we will be able to get home again.'

Kelvin stood up and said, 'I'm the timekeeper, and it's my responsibility to make sure we get home in time and safely. We have already been here nine hours, two minutes and twelve, thirteen seconds, so our time here is running out very fast.' Everybody turned and looked at Kelvin. He went bright red and walked out of the room.

Grandma turned to Ivan and Flora and said, 'Please excuse me. I need to speak to Kelvin,' and she went after him.

Yazz said, 'Please excuse me,' and they had both left the room, leaving me and Fred. Witch Matilda walked over to me and whispered in my ear, 'Max, remember who worked out that the missing children belonged to Winston?'

I knew exactly what Witch Matilda meant. I looked at Flora and said, 'Please don't be annoyed with my grandma. It was me who worked out that the missing children belonged to Winston. My grandma believes that she is doing the right thing. Your father is getting very old.'

Flora looked at me, and I could see her eyes were filled with tears. She turned to Ivan and he wrapped his arms around her. I felt very guilty. I had a terrible sick feeling and I felt cold air all around me, which was the guilt I felt for Flora and Grandma right now. I walked over to Flora and said, 'Please forgive me.'

Flora held my hand and said, 'You haven't done anything wrong, young man, and I can understand that your grandma has followed her heart. The situation is nobody's fault. It was an accident. Me and my sister Stella were told many, many times not to go near the secret gate. We were only young nine and seven, and like all children we wanted to explore, so curiosity got the better of us. We tried many times to get back, but it was impossible for us to return. The consequences of our curiosity have been a burden ever since that day.' Flora now had tears running down her face. She looked at Fred and said, 'You have mentioned my father but not my mother. Please tell me about my mother.'

Fred paused and took a deep breath. A look of deep sadness came over his face like I had never seen before. Fred looked straight at Flora and just shook his head from side to side. Flora had a look of disbelief on her face. Fred said, 'I'm really sorry, Flora. There isn't much I can tell you, because your father, while a very well respected man within the village, is also a very secret man who likes to keep to himself. But what I do know is … your mother is no longer with us. In our village, you and your sister are known as the missing children, or lost children. Your father keeps everything close to his heart, and who can blame him after losing you and your sister. In order to find out if the missing children were Winston's, we needed to travel to Horsey Gap and visit Witch Matilda in her alcazar, and ask her if the lost children belonged to Winston, because nobody knew the answer. Daisy even went to Winston's house and asked him directly before we started the journey. Winston gave no reply, but Daisy wouldn't accept this – she wanted to know. It's been a long journey to get to you, and we have overcome many obstacles, travelled through time, and nothing has stopped Daisy from getting to you. In her heart, Daisy believes it's the least she can do.'

Flora asked, 'Why hasn't my father come with you?'

Fred paused for a moment and then replied, 'The short answer is Winston doesn't know we are here.'

Flora didn't like that answer, and I saw anger in her eyes.

Fred said, 'I can explain. The reason for that is because we all decided that we would make sure we could find you and your sister first, to avoid any further upset for your father. The risk now is that we may not have enough time to double back before the passage is closed.'

Flora listened carefully. 'I understand. I know all too well the pain of feeling lost and of being without close family. My father has spent far too much time alone, unlike me and Stella – at least we had each other thanks to Nana

Ada. Fred, I have to inform you that me and my sister decided that once we were married we would never return. Too much time has passed, we both have families of our own, and we will never take any more chances with the secret gate. We lost everything walking through that gate. We cried until we couldn't cry any more. We were very lucky that Nana Ada found us. Nana Ada protected us at all costs. Our first six months here were horrible. People were coming from miles around trying to tell Nana Ada that we were their children and they wanted to take us home. It was so frightening. Almost every day, someone from somewhere that we had never seen would try and claim us for themselves. Nana Ada would not put up with any nonsense. Although Nana Ada already had five children, she treated me and Stella as if we were her own and protected us the same way. Grandpa Sammy is the kindest person you could ever wish to meet, and Mr and Mrs Bones were so good to us – they took us both in and treated us like we were their very own children and protected us the same way Nana Ada did, and this meant we were able to stay together. So you see, this is why we cannot return home.' Flora still had tears streaming down her face.

I asked Flora, 'Are you disappointed that we have come here?'

Flora raised her head and I could the sadness in her eyes. 'I'm not disappointed you are here. I'm just disappointed it's taken so long. But rest assured we have had a good life, and I would like you to reassure my father of that in case I never see him again.'

I told Flora, 'Witch Matilda has been trying to get you home from the moment you left, but without the timekeeper, it was impossible.'

Flora asked, 'Who is the timekeeper?'

'Kelvin is the timekeeper. He keeps time all around the world, just by looking at the time from any clock, even that clock there,' and I pointed to the clock on the wall, 'Kelvin will look at that and work out the time anywhere in the world in a split second.'

'How wonderful.'

'Yes. Kelvin loves tracking time, so that's why we were able to visit, so we are guaranteed a safe passage home.' In the corner of my eye, Witch Matilda was coming into view. I slowly turned around, so as not to distract anyone, to look at Witch Matilda. I could see she was very upset. She whispered in my ear, 'Ask if Stella is coming.'

'Flora, may I ask, is Stella coming?'

'Stella is not able to come right now. She's busy with her funfair.'

Is that Stella's funfair at the end of St Anne's Road?

'Yes, that's correct. Have you seen the funfair?'

'Yes,' I replied.

Fred told Flora that he thought the funfair was very well presented, and Flora said, 'Yes, Stella and her family work day and night to keep it up to that standard.'

Fred replied, 'It's worth it. Did you say Stella lives in a caravan the whole year round?'

'Yes,' Stella said. 'Sometimes I tease Stella that she only married into the funfair industry because she loves living in a caravan. She hasn't got time to live in a house, it's too much upkeep, and she doesn't have time, because running and maintaining the funfair takes up all her time.'

It was then that Mr Hackman returned with the tea. It seemed like he'd been gone for a long time, and he explained, 'Sorry it's taken so long. We ran out of tea.'

Fred asked Mr Hackman, 'Did you see Daisy out there?'

'Arr. Her said her will be back in a few minutes. Young Kelvin am a bit upset, by the looks of things, and he wants to go home. If yo don't mind me asking, am young Kelvin all right?'

I said, 'Yes, Kelvin is fine, but he's autistic.'

Mr Hackman said, 'Autistic? What's that?'

'You can call it a social disorder. Kelvin struggles around any people he doesn't know, and he only likes routine and calm, and anything out of his routine can cause him to get upset. This journey has been a struggle for him, although he has managed well very up to now.'

Flora asked, 'Is there anything we can do?'

'Yes, just be quiet when he walks back into the room.'

Mr Hackman gave everybody a cup of tea, and then Grandma, Yazz and Kelvin came back into the room and sat down quietly.

'Sorry about that,' said Grandma. 'Kelvin just needed some fresh air.'

Once all the tea was gone, Flora told Grandma, 'My sister and I will not be returning. This is our home now, and I understand that your time here is limited, and I'm grateful that you have travelled all this way, and I do not want you to miss your passage home. I'm sorry for wasting your time.'

Grandma looked at Flora and said, 'I understand. I knew that would be the outcome after talking to Mr Hackman. Your father spends almost every minute of his life in the walled garden and I can only assume he's been waiting for you and your sister to arrive home. So, can I just ask what are we to do about your father?'

Flora's eyes started to fill with tears again. 'I love my father and mother, and every day since we left, I think of them.

Then Ivan, who had not muttered one word, said, 'Do yo think Winston would come and live here with us? We have a three-bedroom house and a large garden. Ar understand it would be a big change, but if he am of a great age, let's be totally honest – he's not going to live forever.'

Flora had a look of excitement on her face. Grandma replied, 'That's one of the best ideas I have heard so far. Winston appears to live a simple life, so I don't think that the year, be it 2017 or 1931, will make much difference to him.'

Fred said, 'Winston likes his garden and he likes his caravan, both of which you have. It sounds like the perfect solution.'

I looked over at Witch Matilda and I could see she was in deep thought. She walked over to Kelvin and Grandma and whispered in their ears. Both Daisy and Kelvin got up and murmured, 'Please excuse us again,' and then walked out.

Flora seemed to have calmed down and her mood had lightened.

Fred asked Flora, 'Stella has two children, is the correct?'

'Yes. Clara, who's twelve, and Ruby, who's nine.'

'How do they get on with school, what with the funfair moving around?'

'Most of the time, the fair is in this area, and if it goes far away, the girls stay with me through the week.' Flora glanced out the door thoughtfully. 'Is the young lad alright?'

I remembered that Flora and Ivan couldn't see Witch Matilda so were probably wondering why they'd gone out again. 'Yes, I'm sure they're fine,' I said.

Fred was obviously thinking the same thing because he said, 'Max, would you go and see if everything is all right?'

'Yes, of course.'

As I walked out of the back room and through the corridor I couldn't see them, so I wandered outside, and there they were: Grandma was in deep conversation with Witch Matilda, and as I approached I could hear Grandma saying, 'Winston will not live forever.'

Witch Matilda replied, 'I'm aware of that, and I would love Winston to be reunited with his daughters, but what if he will not make the change and we have to come and tell Flora and Stella their father doesn't want to come and live here?'

Grandma replied, 'Well, in that case, we are back to that big, long word: consequences. That's the chance we will have to take. This journey has been one long chance. The only question here is, can we get Winston back here in time?'

Witch Matilda looked at Kelvin and said, 'Give me the stats on the time, please.'

Kelvin said, 'We have been here nine hours, sixteen minutes and forty-one, forty-two seconds, leaving us two, hours thirty-one minutes, forty-six seconds with the allowance of twelve minutes, thirty-two seconds to get back to the Royal Electric Theatre.'

Witch Matilda replied, 'Excellent job, Kelvin. If we leave now, we can get back to the walled garden and back here before our twelve hours is up – but we have to work fast if this is going to work, and before we leave you must tell Flora that it's a race against time, and she must meet us with her sister at the Royal Electric Theatre at precisely 18.00. Also, make sure you make it crystal clear that if we have not returned by eighteen sixteen, then we couldn't convince Winston to make the move and there is no guarantee that we will return. That way, we can be sure they are not wasting their time – but please hurry.'

Kelvin, Grandma and I hurried back into the Anchor

Hotel. Daisy looked straight at Flora and Ivan and said, 'I'm really sorry, but we've got to leave now if we are going to get your father back before our safe passage is closed. However, we cannot guarantee that we can make it back again in time, so this is my instruction: you and your sister must be waiting for us at the stage door entrance at precisely 18.00, and if we have not returned by sixteen minutes past, that means that we are not returning, definitely not returning – not tomorrow, not next week, so please do not waste your time waiting – that you must promise me. If we can get back here, it's today only.'

Flora said, 'Please, just to be clear, you said precisely 18.16. I don't know what that means.'

Kelvin said, 'Yes, of course. A twenty-four-hour clock is still a bit too modern for 1931. So, your time will quarter past six in the evening, and if we have not arrived by sixteen minutes past, that means we are not returning.'

We said our goodbyes and quickly left. Kelvin looked much happier that finally we were moving. He told us that we had now been there for nine hours and twenty-five minutes and sixteen seconds, and that the current time in Cradley Heath was 3.25 p.m., and that when we arrived it was 6.15 a.m., so we went back in time, meaning clock time, so when we would arrive back in the walled garden it would be 03.25.

'Yes, that's correct, Kelvin,' Grandma replied when he'd finished.

'That means Winston will be in bed, Grandma.'

'Not if I've got anything to do with it.'

Witch Matilda told Grandma, 'We have done well so far. Please do not let the success get the better of you. Remember, Winston is a secret man and will not tolerate drama or fuss.'

As we turned the corner into Bank Street, the loud bang, bang was still going on. Then we arrived back at the Royal Electric Theatre.

Kelvin said. 'Perfect. Just as I predicted, twelve minutes thirty seconds.'

Arthur was waiting for us, and we quickly changed out of our 1930s clothing. Arthur told us, 'I've spoken to Mrs Dawson, and she advised me to do everything I can to help you.'

Daisy replied, 'That's very kind, and we are truly grateful.'

Arthur asked, 'Have you been successful?'

Daisy replied, 'That depends on the next couple of hours. We are going to try and return, so please can you wait here until 6.20 p.m.?'

'Yes, of course.'

We said our goodbyes, and Grandma added, 'Just in case we do not return, we would all like to thank you, Arthur, for all your support.'

Once changed, we all lined up. Witch Matilda was first in line, then Kelvin, Yazz, me, Grandma, and Fred was last. Kelvin made sure we were all ready and told us to hold hands. Then he checked the time: it was 15.47. Kelvin insisted that we wait until exactly 15.50 to avoid confusion. And then the time came, and Witch Matilda pulled the door, and we all hoped that we were going to step into the walled garden.

Walking back through the secret gate seemed to take a while longer, and it seemed much darker. Kelvin was timing the journey back. He knew that it had only taken 2.6 seconds for us all to get through. This time Kelvin said, 'It's taking longer! Keep walking!'

Witch Matilda said, 'Don't stop!'

For a few seconds, it felt like we had made a mistake, then finally we stepped back into the walled garden. Kelvin said, 'That took exactly double the amount of time – 5.2 seconds.'

Witch Matilda said, 'Quick as you can, Kelvin, how much time do we have?'

'Two hours, nine minutes and 44.8 seconds.'

'Well done, Kelvin. Without you, none of this would be possible.' Kelvin was delighted.

We all gathered ourselves and started to look around, and as we were about to walk back down the steps, much to our surprise, Winston was there, standing looking up at us. We all stopped, still and silent. There was an air of guilt hanging over us, and I felt as though if I lifted my hands in the air I would be able to touch the guilt. Winston was holding this moment, and the whole future, in the palm of his hands.

I thought to myself, how can a man that doesn't say very much have so much power? The power to stop us talking, the power to make us stand to attention without uttering one word – and yet that was precisely the situation. Nobody dared move or even turn our heads. We were like soldiers.

Winston looked at Witch Matilda and asked, 'Have you found my girls?'

Witch Matilda said, 'I can explain.'

Then, in a slightly higher tone of voice, Winston repeated, 'Have you found my girls?'

Witch Matilda said, 'Yes we have.'

And with the silence broken, we all felt like we could move again. We slowly started to walk down the steps. As we moved closer to Winston, I could see his eyes were filling with tears.

'Please tell me, are my girls safe and well?'

Witch Matilda replied, 'Very well and very safe.'

A smile slowly appeared on Winston's face.

Witch Matilda carried on. 'Flora has two boys, and Stella has two girls.'

And then, much to our surprise, Winston asked if there was any possibility that he could see the girls.

Witch Matilda replied, 'You can go and live with them if you would like to.'

Winston replied, 'Who will look after the garden?'

Witch Matilda said, 'That will not be your problem. I will make sure the garden is well looked after. I have to tell you we only have a short time to get you there. The passage will soon close. Also, once you go through, you will be living in 1931.'

Winston replied, 'That will make no difference to me. I was aware of what you have all been doing today, and because so much time had passed, I expected that it would be me leaving, and not my girls returning. This could be the only answer, and I'm ready to be reunited with my family. I have missed my girls every day of my life since they left, and once my wife passed away, I have spent as much time as possible in this garden, praying my girls would come back to me.'

I looked around, and Grandma and Yazz were crying. Fred had tears in his eyes too.

Winston gestured to the floor by his feet and I saw his bag. He was ready to leave, his bag packed.

Grandma asked, 'Is that all you need?'

Winston replied, 'You can all see that I'm very old, and I'm not going to live forever. Material things don't mean anything to me. So long as I have a garden and my tools and a few changes of clothes, that's all I need.'

Witch Matilda said, 'Is there anybody you would like to say goodbye to?'

Winston replied, 'I've already done that.'

Kelvin said, 'Time is getting on. Let's make a move.'

With that, we all turned around and once again were ready to walk through the secret gate, except this time we had Winston.

Kelvin said, 'The time is four thirty-eight, so please wait two minutes, until precisely four forty.'

Winston told Kelvin that he was doing a very good job.

When it was time, we all held hands and made our way through the secret gate again. It seemed to be taking longer.

Witch Matilda said, 'This passage will soon close. We must be quick!'

And then, after what seemed much longer than the last time, we were back in the Royal Electric Theatre, and to our delight Arthur was waiting for us. 'Hello,' he said. 'It's nice to see you again.'

Winston looked somewhat startled.

Grandma told him, 'Don't worry. You're safe now. We are in the Royal Electric Theatre, Cradley Heath, the heart of the Black Country. One of the best places I have ever visited in 1931.'

Fred told Winston, 'The people are really friendly. It's a lovely place.'

Winston walked over to Grandma and said, 'I would like to thank you for what you have done, and I apologise for my behaviour when you came to my house. You are a very brave, unselfish woman, and your family are very lucky to have you. If I could stand here thanking you for the rest of the day, that would still not be enough.'

Winston walked over to Fred and told him, 'I'm sure you have been a great support on this journey for Daisy. I for one was relieved when Mr Fudge told me that you had gone with Daisy. I'm sure your old friend Jim would very proud of you.'

Winston walked over to Kelvin and told him, 'Without you, the timekeeper, none of this would have been possible. You have done an amazing job, and I thank you from the bottom of my heart.'

Next, he addressed Yazz. 'Yazz, I would like to thank you, as, well, I'm sure that you have played your part, even if it was just going along for the ride because Daisy would never have left you behind.'

Then he looked at me. 'And now, you, Young Max. I'm sure you have learnt many things from this journey. I know you are a wise young man, and again without you the journey may not have happened if you hadn't worked out that the missing children were my girls, so thank you for being so thoughtful and having consideration for me.'

We all stood again in silence as if we were listening to our commanding officer.

Fred said, 'Winston, you have said more to us in the last fifteen minutes than in all the years I've known you.'

Winston replied, 'I don't say much, but I see everything. Sometimes there are things that have to be said, and this, Fred, is just one of these occasions. Last but not least, Witch Matilda—'

At this, Arthur came to life. 'Witch? Where is the witch? You never mentioned a witch last time!' He'd gone white with fear. We had forgotten to tell Winston that Witch Matilda is not visible to anybody else except us.'

Grandma said, 'Don't worry, Arthur. Witch Matilda is a very kind witch.'

'Can I ask, where is Witch Matilda? Because from where I'm standing, I cannot see any witch.'

'No, Witch Matilda is only visible to us, but she is in the room, and Witch Matilda can hear every word you're saying.'

'I'm really sorry, but I've never been in the company of a witch before.'

I wished Arthur could see Witch Matilda and see how beautiful she was.

Arthur had calmed down, so Winston carried on. 'Witch Matilda, thank you for allowing me to live in your house and for letting me look after the walled garden. Because of the garden, I have lived a long, healthy life, making sure that I eat healthy food.'

Winston turned once again to me, Kelvin and Yazz and said, 'If anybody ever tells you work never hurt anybody, I'm living proof of that. Just make sure you eat well. Now, I have one more thing to do before I leave – my keys. Who will take the keys to the house and the walled garden?'

'Daisy, would you like them?' Witch Matilda said.

Grandma was lost for words, and Yazz, Kelvin and I were overwhelmed with happiness. We couldn't believe that our grandma would be living there next.

Fred had a big smile on his face. 'Daisy, you said you wanted to move back to the village.'

Grandma paused for a moment and then said, in the most excited tone of voice, 'Yes! Yes, of course! Yes!'

I shouted out, 'Yes, Grandma! You will be living next door!'

Witch Matilda said, 'There is one big issue, and it comes with—'

'Don't tell me,' said Grandma. 'Consequences.'

Witch Matilda smiled and said, 'You are a wise woman.'

Arthur said, 'Please tell me everything is going well, because I'm only hearing one side of the conversation.'

And then with the most beautiful glow of green the room lit up, and Arthur was looking in amazement as Witch Matilda had made herself visible. Arthur had a look of disbelief on his face, mouth wide open. He never said one word. Witch Matilda said all is well.

Then Witch Matilda looked at Arthur and said, 'Thank you for your help today.'

For some reason, Arthur did a gentle bow. It was as if he had just met the Queen.

Witch Matilda said, 'Come now, Winston. Your girls will be waiting for you. Kelvin – time left, please?'

'The time here is 17.17. We have exactly fifty-eight minutes left,' Kelvin said.

We all walked towards the stage door. Arthur quickly got in front so that he could open it for us. Witch Matilda led the way through the door, and Arthur bowed his head again as Witch Matilda passed him.

As we all stepped out onto Bank Street, Witch Matilda was once again out of sight. It was very quiet – the banging had finally stopped.

Winston looked around and said, 'Where do we go from here?'

Witch Matilda said, 'Nowhere. Your girls will be here soon.'

After a few minutes, Winston started to get anxious. Grandma told Winston, 'They will be here soon. I told them to be here at precisely 6.15 p.m., so we have plenty of time.'

We were all standing quietly, and every minute seemed like an hour.'

Winston told Grandma, 'I have left you clear instructions step by step, and a day-by-day diary so you know what will need to be done each day of the week and when to take a few days away without anything getting ruined.' Then Winston turned to me, Kelvin and Yazz and said, 'Your wish has come true. Can I trust you three to help your grandma to look after the walled garden?'

'YES!' we said in unison with an excited tone of voice.

Winston nodded and said, 'Very good.'

Then Grandma said, 'Shhh a minute. I can hear something.' And she was right – we could hear the voices of people coming towards us. As we all turned to look up Bank Street, we saw Flora and Ivan, accompanied by another young couple, who we could only assume to be Stella and her husband. As they got nearer, Flora and Stella started to walk faster, leaving the men behind.

Winston also started walking forward, then he dropped his bag and opened his arms.

Flora and Stella started to run down the street towards their father, and then they all came together in the most incredible embrace. Everybody was crying – Bank Street was a flood of tears. Winston was crying, 'The girls! My girls! My beautiful girls! I have missed you so much, I have waited for you to return every day since you left!'

Flora introduced us to Stella, and her husband Leonard.

Flora and Stella turned to us, and Stella said, 'We cannot thank you enough. Thank you so much for bringing our father to us. We will look after him.'

Grandma replied, 'It's been a very tough journey at times, with some very difficult decisions to make, and hopefully you will never be in the same position. We are very pleased to see you reunited with your father. We are all happy to have played a part in putting you all back together. I'm really sorry it's taken so long.'

Flora said, 'It's taken a long time but, it's not too late.'

Grandma said, 'Now, sorry, but we must be off soon – time is ticking away.'

Flora replied, 'Yes, yes of course. Please don't miss your passage.'

There was one big hug and we all shook hands, and then it was time for us to leave.

Witch Matilda said, 'Kelvin, time please.'

'18.09.'

Arthur quickly opened to stage door. I looked back to take one last look at Winston, and it was a beautiful sight: both Flora and Stella were still embracing their father as they walked up Bank Street. And then I turned to walk back into the Royal Electric Theatre.

Arthur said, 'I'm going to miss you. Today has been the most interesting day of my life. The sad part is nobody except Mrs Dawson is going to believe me, especially if I tell them I met a witch.'

Grandma said, 'Life can be a strange place. It's been lovely to meet you, Arthur. Thanks for all your help.'

We all lined up again. Kelvin shouted, 'There's no time left! We must go now.' Off we went, and a few seconds later we were back in the walled garden.

We looked around, gathered ourselves together and walked back down the stairs. Witch Matilda locked the secret gate, and that signalled the end of our day. I felt so sad that it was also time for Witch Matilda to leave.

Witch Matilda said, 'Well, your journey has ended. Daisy, Fred, Yazz, Kelvin and Max, you have all done a very good job – especially you, Kelvin. Without you, it would have been impossible. You are a very nice young man with an amazing talent. Keep up the good work.'

Kelvin was glowing. He thanked Witch Matilda for allowing him the opportunity to be the timekeeper.

'Max, without your realisation, the journey wouldn't have started. You are a wise young man. And Yazz, you have been a great support. Fred, as Winston said, Jim would be very proud of you. Daisy, you are an incredible person, dedicated to your family, and because of your dedication, you felt it very important to help Winston. Your strength is your family, and now you will be able to live next door for the rest of your life.'

Grandma nodded deeply in thanks.

Witch Matilda went on, 'And now we must part, but remember, the birds are always watching. Take care.' With that, Witch Matilda climbed onto her broomstick, and the black crow with the green eyes perched himself on the broomstick, and off they went.

We made our way out of the walled garden. Grandma locked up, and we all walked back up the purple path without fear. It was 06.25 now, and we all said goodnight to Fred, even though it was daylight. As we got back to our house, Mum and Dad pulled up in their car. We were all so pleased to see them.

I gave Mum the biggest, tightest hug ever. Dad said, 'We decided to come back because nobody was answering the phone.'

I told Dad, 'We are pleased that you are home.'

Dad looked at us and said, Have you been up all night?'

Grandma replied, 'Something like that.'

We were all so tired, so we stood in contented silence, our minds buzzing.

Finally, Dad said, 'So, can someone please tell what you've been up to?'

I told Dad, 'It's a very long story. I'll tell you tomorrow. Promise.'

The End